The Strange Case of the Missing Bridge
A Zeb Dasher Mystery Novel

The Strange Case of the Missing Bridge

Dr. Myron Baughman

Published by Myron Baughman, 2024.

While every precaution has been taken in the preparation of this book, the publisher assumes no responsibility for errors or omissions, or for damages resulting from the use of the information contained herein.

THE STRANGE CASE OF THE MISSING BRIDGE

First edition. June 24, 2024.

ISBN: 979-8227451484

Written by Dr. Myron Baughman.

Also by Dr. Myron Baughman

The Strange Case of the Missing Bridge

Watch for more at https://www.sermonaudio.com/ source_detail.asp?sourceid=kingjamesseminary.

This Book is Dedicated to my loving wife Denise.

By Dr. Myron Baughman

Dedicated to My Loving Wife Denise

Table of Contents

1.

One Foggy Night

My name is Zeb Dasher, internationally renowned investigator. I have been a private investigator for a little over twenty years in North West Pennsylvania. My home is in the little town of Clarion with a population of around seven thousand people. It has a teacher's college, soon to be upgraded to a university. The main industry in Clarion was the Owens-Illinois Glass Factory. I must tell you a few other background facts before we get started with this case. This is necessary so to give a clearer and more complete picture of the entire case.

I do have practical credentials for my work besides degrees in criminal justice and investigation. I did work for the Pittsburgh Police Department as a detective. I have investigated many things and many people. I made national headlines several times. Once I cracked an espionage case for the federal government that involved a powerful senator leaking government secrets to enemy agents in D.C. I usually do not travel out of state, but wherever the leads take me, I must go. I also investigated the murder of a New York millionaire. I had to travel not just to New York, but also to several places overseas since these people were jetsetters. It turned out that it was his wife that had him murdered by a hit man. I think my biggest case was investigating the stolen diamond necklace that was on maximum-security display in the Pittsburgh Museum. I do not know, though, the missing tiara of Queen

Elizabeth was also a big case. That seemed to be an easy case, since I was able to solve in a week's time, so no matter.

The Clarion River has a dam on it called the Piney Dam that makes the river a hundred feet deep. The Clarion River Bridge on Route 322 has spanned that river for many years. It was inspected and passed by the PA. DOT (or PENNDOT) a month before this incident happened. I have been over that steel bridge many times, with no thoughts of any problem with the bridge. There have been many trucks and tractor-trailers over that bridge since it was first constructed. Since the bridge passed the safety inspection, there was no doubt in anyone's mind that the bridge was safe. As a precaution, those trucks with extremely heavy loads, by-pass it and go to the heavy duty bridge on the newly constructed Interstate 80. It was a detour of considerable distance, and some truck drivers ignored that advice.

Some of the following details not even the police had in their investigation. I now share these with you.

It took place very late on the last day of March 1969, in the early hours of the morning. It was a normal day. People had passed over the Clarion River Bridge without incident all that day. There were fishermen along the banks of the river most of the day, as usual. People came to the natural spring that was at the base of the river hill all day to fill their glass milk containers with fresh spring water. They noticed nothing unusual. After about eight o'clock in the evening people, stopped coming to the spring, and the fishermen all went home. Heavy fog began to settle over the area. Some people were to return early the next morning, however. As I said, during the evening and then late that night, heavy, dense fog settled in, especially around the river. This is an important factor in the case. It slowed all traffic in the area to a crawl. Even traffic on Main Street, Clarion came to almost a halt. Obviously, it was time for everyone to be home, safe in bed.

In the wee hours of the morning, one long distance truck driver who was carrying an extremely heavy load rolled slowly and quietly through town. The over-sized load was draped with a thick tarp. There were two armed escort trucks accompanying the tractor-trailer. One was in the front, the lead, and then, there was one in the rear. Both had flashing blue lights. Even though they could still read the large heavy load detour sign through the fog, they never the less continued their journey on 322 through town. The town itself was empty of occupants at that time of night. Since the fog stopped practically everyone from even going outside earlier, much less drive, the streets were deserted of traffic. The truck went slowly down the river hill. The truck driver had to down shift to a very low gear for the descent down the steep hill. At the bottom of the hill, the road made a sharp right turn to go on to the bridge. The lead escort truck went on first, and then the big truck slowly went on, followed by the last escort truck. Just as they were in the middle of the bridge, the whole thing collapsed into the deep river. The entire structure disappeared below the surface, leaving only the two large stone supports standing. Besides the supports, everything was gone. The tractor-trailer and the escort trucks were gone also.

2.
Stumping Investigators

Early the next morning, the police, and then the state police were called to investigate the strange sight of the missing bridge. It was considered to have collapsed some time during the night and sank to the bottom of the river. When the deep-water divers were sent down to investigate below the water level, they came up empty handed. They reported that there was absolutely nothing down at the bottom. Then, they came up with the idea that maybe, just by some freak accident, the bridge had been carried by the current downstream. This was highly unlikely because the current was slow moving and not viewed to be strong enough to move anything the size of a large bridge made out of steel. The weight of the bridge was figured to be more than what could be lifted out of the water by local means. Once found, the bridge would possibly have to be cut into sections, and raised. They would use inflation devices for that.

The authorities sent their divers downstream all the way to the dam, miles away, and reported nothing. They sent metal detectors and used sonar to find the bridge in the following days, and still came up with nothing. They even went upstream, looking, but gave up. The conclusion was that the bridge was stolen! Yes, stolen! The police were made laughing stocks for that conclusion, so the state sent in their own special investigators.

The state sent a team of six well-trained and experienced men. They took several weeks looking into the matter in considerable detail. Possible eyewitnesses were interviewed, but no new substantial evidence was uncovered. There was no one out that night. Visibility was very poor. Even if there were pictures, it was argued that they would not show much. Finally, after weeks of fruitless searching and investigative hours spent, the whole case was at a standstill. It was in danger of being a cold case when it was decided to be sent to the FBI in Washington, D.C. Construction on a new bridge was delayed because the missing bridge represented a possible crime scene of mysterious proportions.

Some argued that it could not be a crime scene. As in a murder investigation, if there is no body, then it is difficult to prove a crime had been committed. That, in itself was ridiculous logic. The question was who would want the bridge anyways, even if it could be stolen. Logically there is no way to actually steal a bridge because of its size and weight, so the idea of the incident being a crime was thrown out. It became an unsolved mystery.

Then, another important question that went unanswered, was the question as to whether there was anyone missing along with the bridge. According to the special investigators from DC, the major trucking companies reported no trucks missing. No truck was scheduled to have crossed that bridge for almost a week. Most trucking companies used the detour around the bridge. Only light loads had crossed the bridge within a week's time of it disappearing. No one reported seeing anything strange going on that night either. The fog was the only thing of note that night, which was a fact that only left the FBI investigators in a fog.

Next, the question about was anything from the air seen by a passing airplane or jet. The answer to that question was shortly concluded. Cloud cover that night was so thick; nothing could have been seen from the air. There were no commercial planes or jets directly overhead during the entire night according to the FAA. No private plane was in the air overhead that entire night, either. So there were no eye witnesses from the sky to question.

Sadly, the whole thing became a joke. Some jokesters put ads in the newspaper advertising a bridge for sale. Some even put up billboards advertising the town as a tourist attraction for having the only stolen bridge in the world. Commercial vendors appeared selling souvenirs showing the bridge on cups and china plates. One large billboard that appeared just outside of town said, "Have you seen this bridge? It displayed the bridge below the wording. Another billboard asked, "It's ten o'clock, do you know where your bridge is at?" It would have been funny had it not been disturbing to some of the people who lived there. It did draw in people from all over the world. Sightseers came with their cameras to see an empty place where the road stopped at the river. So, the tourists were coming to actually see nothing. Downtown merchants quickly caught on and petitioned the state not to replace the missing bridge. This idea was dismissed since there were people who lived on the other side of the bridge who did not like to have to take a long detour to get into town.

The mystery remained unsolved and left untouched for several years, while a plan of action concerning the bridge and the construction of a new one was under debate. It was considered to be wise to move the new bridge a little farther up the hill, and leave the empty place where the old one once stool alone. People could still come and stare at nothing and take pictures of the empty space. The only good thing that they could get from going all the way, down to where the missing bridge once stood was that they could still get fresh spring water for free.

Then a newly elected town council met and demanded answers of just what exactly happen to their bridge. It was an unsolved mystery, and they felt as if the police failed them in something that should have been obvious. Some on the council warned that if the real answer were ever found, then the tourists would stop coming. The council compromised and did not demand anything right away, but they did want the matter to come to a quiet logical conclusion. It was to be quietly revealed to the city council, but kept hush hush to the newspapers. This is when they turned to me, Zeb Dasher, solver of deep mysteries.

3.

Zeb Dasher to Assist

I WAS FIRST CALLED by phone to the new City Council Meeting. There, they desired to discuss the case with me to see if I wanted to actually take it. Before going into the meeting, I knew I would take the case, but at a price. I would not accept a case that no one else could solve without a good and proper reward for my efforts. I would be fair with my price. I never set the price on how long it takes me to solve the case, since some cases may take months, or even years I had no doubt in my mind that I could solve the case even though the best had already tried. I was an unusual investigator. I had the habit of looking where no one else looked, as well as having unusual investigative techniques and style.

When I walked into the council room, they were all sitting at a long table, most were businessmen of the local area. I recognized most of them. A few of them were out of town investors. One investor was interested in building a new hotel in Clarion to accommodate the tourists. The new council members generally felt that the story of the missing bridge was good for the community and they did not want that to be destroyed by my investigation. They also felt at the same time, that they wanted to know the truth. So, they were interested in hiring me to get to the bottom of it.

"So, Mr. Dasher, how do you propose to solve this mystery when everyone else failed?" the spokesman of the group began.

"I intend on investigating it."

"We know that, sir, but just what do you plan on doing differently than the others? You know not even the FBI came up with any answers."

"I can't tell you that yet since I don't know what all they have done to solve this case. I can give you progress reports as I go along if you like."

"You first answers aren't very impressive, I'm afraid," one council member remarked.

"Well, if you ask a stupid question, you will get a stupid answer. That is how it goes. Now, I will solve this case, and inform you privately the conclusion. I promise you that. I also need paid for my fine services. I can solve cases, as you know, that no one else can, including the FBI."

"Okay, just exactly what do you want for you so called fine services?" one council member asked.

"Fifty thousand dollars."

"What? Did I just hear you say fifty thousand dollars?" the council spokesman sputtered.

"Yes, and I'm giving you a discount."

The council members all became quiet and looked at each other.

"Thank you for your time, Mr. Dasher. That will be all for now. If we decide that this thing is worth fifty thousand dollars, we will call you."

"That will be okay by me, but remember, I am at high demand. If I am on another case, you will have to wait until I can get to your request if you ever decide that you want me to solve it for you. I take one case at a time. Let me remind you that I have a one hundred percent success rate. No other investigator with over twenty years of experience can make that claim. I have no unsolved, cold cases. Good luck, gentlemen." I said, handed them one of my business cards and then I walked out.

Early the next morning, I received a phone call from the council asking me to come back in. I had just got off the phone with a different prospective client when the council called. Since I had not been commissioned yet, I was free to still speak with the council. I met them again at ten o'clock that morning.

"Good morning, sir, won't you have a seat," the spokesman said.

"That will be alright," I said and sat down in a soft, leather chair opposite the spokesman. "I take it that you have reconsidered."

"Yes, we have decided to hire you, but not at fifty thousand dollars."

"Sorry, the price is non-negotiable. I take fifty percent up front, and then after the case is solved, I collect the other fifty percent."

"We were prepared to negotiate, but since that is off the table right away, then maybe, we really have nothing to discuss with you," the spokesman said, Then, suddenly, a man to his right, put his hand over the spokesman's hand, and said.

"I think we will agree to his terms after all. This whole thing has been hanging over our heads for years now. It is best that we go ahead and put it to rest. We will have an official answer."

"We already have an official answer, it is a mystery. That is what the tourists come to see for themselves."

"That is true. We need to be informed with the real truth. History isn't healthy left hanging." One council member stood up and said.

"Yes, but we don't want to hurt the flourishing tourist trade, now do we? I say, we live with it and keep our fifty thousand dollars." Another member said.

"Let's play it safe. If word got that we knew the answer to the mystery, no one would trust us. We might even get voted out of office," another member said.

"The general public already thinks we know, and we don't." the spokesman said.

"Ignorance will make fools of us all. Hire the man!" another council member stood up and demanded. They looked at each other quietly, and then each one nodded.

"Yes, you have a deal. We will have the city bank draw up the check for you this afternoon. Come back here at two thirty this afternoon, and you will have your check," the spokesman said.

I went to lunch at the Clarion Clipper Restaurant and over ate. I tend to do that before I start another big case. My ex-wife always remarked at my ability to stay thin even though I ate at just one meal more than most humans eat during the entire day. Maybe it was sort of a celebration thing with me to eat like that before starting a new case. Maybe it was just a bad habit. Two thirty came around shortly after I finished my nice meal. I went back to the council room in the courthouse and found them all waiting.

"Yes, Mr. Dasher, we are ready for you. Along with this check, we will need you to sign this contract agreement. We will be expecting feedback from you on a regular basis," the spokesman said and pointed me to the paper on the table for me to sign.

"I must read it first. Hmmn, it looks to be a simple, standard agreement," I said glancing over it, before I signed it. "I have my own contract, which my attorney has drawn up, but this will be fine. If nothing else, your cashed check is contract enough to be legal." I said and signed the contract.

"Fine, then its official. When will you begin your investigation?"

"Oh, it has already started with this check. I need to ask some questions, privately of one or two of the council members, in particular, of the ones who didn't want this case solved."

"Really? I must say, that seems to be highly irregular. After all, we all agreed to hire you." One of the members protested.

"Some of us are under suspicion? I find that to be ridiculous." Another member said.

"I did not say anything about suspicion, however, you agreed to my methods with this check. I will begin here."

"What would any of us do with a bridge? I find this to be outrageous," another member said.

"Make money off of it, that is motivation, sir," I replied.

"How ridiculous!" another member said.

"Let me start with you, since you are protesting the loudest. Come, do we have a room that we can meet in privately?"

"Yes, just next door to this one. There is no one in there at this time," the council spokesman said.

"Come, after you sir," I said and pointed the council member to the door. We walked to the next room, and sat down at a large mahogany table.

Your name sir," I began. "For the record."

"Edward Hopness."

"Why do you not want this case solved?"

"Like I said back there, it may cost the town its tourist attraction."

"So, you propose that you are looking out for the town. Is that true?"

"Absolutely."

"Is it not also true that you were struggling to keep your business afloat before the bridge disappeared?"

"Every business has ups and downs."

"Yes, but now you are looking at million dollar proposed projects."

"Yes, a man must grab opportunities when they come along, and use them to his advantage. There is nothing criminal about that."

"It may be criminal if it ends up that it costs the state, and as a consequence the tax payer, millions of dollars to replace a bridge that you had something to do with its disappearance."

"Oh, now really? There is nothing to tie me with the disappearance of the bridge, and you know that."

"Really? Did you or did you not get together with two other now council members five years ago, August fifth to be exact, and plot for events that would bring tourists here?"

"Well, yes, but again, there is nothing criminal about trying to make business plans. The Autumn Leaf Festival once a year just was not enough. We all needed more of a boost.

"So, then, just what plans did you come up with?"

"Sales, great prices for a week. That was it, nothing more."

"It was a success?"

"No, it was a flop. It really did not do much for the town at all, especially nothing permanent."

"You agree that a mysterious event would draw the curious here?"

"Well, sure. If you look at some of these places that have reported haunted houses, places around Area 51, and the like, all have tourists."

"So, you all knew that back then, now didn't you?"

"Of course, who doesn't?"

"Are you not one of the citizens here in this county who just a few years ago, claimed that there were Indian ghosts haunting the now college field and track area that lies just at the top of the Clarion River Hill?"

"Well, actually yes."

"It proved to be a hoax didn't it? I mean after some investigations by private citizens, there proved to be no ghosts, ever."

"That is controversial, sir."

"What did you hope to accomplish with that claim?"

"I had no motivation. I was just reporting something that I had seen. Other people had seen them too, you know."

"Yes, but all of them later repudiated their claims, now didn't they?"

"Yes, yes, they did."

"I find this to be strangely similar to the missing bridge case, sir. I do believe there is evidence to show that you were involved in both cases."

"You have nothing that will stand up in a court of law, sir. There has been no crime committed. You are barking up the wrong tree. Now, stop wasting my time."

"Sir, let me warn you, that you just may find yourself to be required to pay the state for the bridge replacement."

"Is that a threat?"

"No, it is just a fact if you had something to do with it."

"Good day, sir. I will be leaving now." The council member got up and left the courthouse. Apparently, he did not like my beginning investigation.

4.

·

The Search for External Clues

THE NEXT DAY, I WENT down to where the old bridge once stood. I did not expect much in the way of obvious clues as to what had happened there years ago. I did have a few tricks up my sleeve, however. I had learned that not all evidence could be seen by the naked eye. So, I brought several tools to look for long lost or originally overlooked things.

First, I got my portable groundmass measuring devise out. What this little marvel would do would measure how compressed the soil was at certain depths. Compressed soil below the surface would indicate heavy equipment had once been there. I had to be careful of the settings so that it did not read so deep as to detect the soil that was compressed when then bridge was first constructed. I also had to factor in erosion, if there was any. Some places gain soil, not lose it, but around riverbanks, erosion is common. After carefully measuring in detail the riverbanks on both sides of the river, the instrument's readings indicated some very heavy equipment had been in the area within the last five to eight years. I would have to confirm the fact that there had been no construction brought into the area in that time frame. I also later confirmed this fact along with the fact that no heavy equipment was actually brought in for any of the investigation procedures. The largest vehicles used in the investigations were only vans, and those never left the pavement.

The next day, I used a metal detector to see if anything had been left behind of the bridge or any other piece of metal that did not belong there. After hours of searching, I did come up a few little things. Less than two feet down, I found one heavy-duty lug nut off a large truck. I judged it to be a military vehicle of at least the ten ton class. On the far bank of the river, I found a real jewel. It was a heavy-duty hook, one that was used for drawing heavy objects up from off the ocean floor. This could have been accidently left behind by a search team. A later investigation told me that there were no search teams that had brought in such equipment since the bridge could not be found. Since this was true, the hook had to have come from whatever caused the bridge to collapse or whatever took the bridge out of the water. The loose theory that the bridge never collapsed and fell in the water had occurred to me. It would be quite a task just to lift the steel bridge off its foundation and into the sky. I found that to be pretty much out of the question, but I did not dismiss the idea entirely.

On the third day, I used the technique familiar with anyone who had done any archeological work; I got my small spade out and a small, hand-held whiskbroom. This was going to be tedious work, but I took my time. I knew I would find evidence, if I was just patient. After five days of investigation using that technique, I found one pocket notebook with nothing written in it. I found one military issue pen. No finger prints. One old green hat that could have been a military style hat, but it was difficult to tell, since there was not much left of it. I found several boot prints still hardened in mud. One was size thirteen, and another one was size sixteen in large men's footwear. These were no midgets who were here previously. I checked boot designs later, and both prints bore the tread design of the military, both air force and the navy. I began to wonder if this then, had been a military operation of some sort. The question that came up in my mind was that if it was, military, then what business did they have with this old bridge? This may prove to be a deeper mystery than what I had anticipated. Obviously, no one in Clarion or in Clarion County had the bridge, or had any reason to have it. The bridge went somewhere. Large steel structures do not just disappear; I just did not have enough leads to take me to it, yet.

Next, I went to Lake Erie and rented a small, personal submarine. It was the only one of its kind in the Great Lakes area. There were similar ones, one in Miami, Florida, and another on the California coast. Both of those were too far away to have shipped, so this one would have to do. I drove up to Erie, PA that next day.

"Is this the place that has a small submarine for rent?" I asked the man sitting on a stool on the wood pier.

"Yes, it is. It is the only one in Pennsylvania. What do you need it for?"

"I am Zeb Dasher, investigator for the Clarion City Council. I am investigating the disappearance of the Clarion River Bridge. I will need your sub to go to the very bottom of the river and look around."

"Well, when you rent the sub, you rent me also. Arnold Kribbs, at your service, sir. I'm the only one that can pilot it, for insurance reasons."

"I understand. Is it available?"

"It most certainly is. It turns out that almost nobody wants to ride in a submarine."

"I understand. So I would like to use it as soon as possible. How much is it?"

"How long are you going to use it?"

"Probably just tomorrow. How deep can this thing go?"

"Measured in feet? A little over one hundred feet down is about it. How deep do you need to go?"

"Not below one hundred feet, probably less."

"Okay, one day at that depth, you will need three thousand dollars."

"Ouch! That is the best you can do?"

"Best for whom? I have a business to run, fella. Take it or leave it."

"Okay, I'll take it. I'll have to leave my vehicle here, and rent a truck to haul it down there."

"You need to get you a professional truck and driver; otherwise it is not leaving the dock here."

"Okay, any idea where I can fill that order?"

"Just down the road. My brother owns a truck rental company, and he has driven trucks for over fifteen years. You will find him to be reasonable."

"Kind of like you?"

"Sure, see Alvin's Truck Rental, on the left, about a quarter of a mile down this same road. Be sure to tell him that I sent you."

"He will give me a discount?"

"Maybe."

After I went down the road and unloaded more of my money, I rented a room at a nearby motel. It was a nice, clean motel, so I did not mind the overnight stay. The next morning, we got an early start. It turned out that I did not need a professional truck driver if I rented one of Alvin's trucks.

When we got to the river site, we did not waste any time getting the sub into the water. This was an expensive project, so I did not want to be charged for another day doing it. It was going to be done today, and that was all there was to it. After the sub was ready, Arnold called me to the hatch and told me to get in. I did, and he showed me how to properly tighten the hatch door above me. It was only a two-seat sub. I certainly felt cramped in the little compartment. Suddenly, I felt the whole thing sink, and me with it. It was not a very pleasant feeling. I had not been very far under the water before, so this was a new experience. Scuba diving was as far under the surface as I ever cared to be, until now. With this thing, I felt trapped inside, whereas with scuba diving, I was in control.

Down we went into the darkness. It soon was pitch dark outside the sub. Arnold switched the outside lights on. Those helped, but the water still appeared dark and gloomy. The further down we went, the less I liked it. To my relief, we soon saw the bottom. There was no sign of a bridge down there, at all. Arnold did a thorough search by moving up and down the bridge area, one narrow section at a time. Suddenly, something appeared out of the ordinary. It looked like a metal beam. We moved the sub in close for a good look. I took out my camera and took pictures of the whole thing. It was a portion of a steel beam. Then, something else appeared to be under the beam.

"Is it possible to get a better look at what is under the beam?" I asked Arnold.

'We can try. I will try to move it with the sub's mechanical arm." Arnold pulled a lever and moved it around. It controlled an arm on the outside of the submarine. He moved in close, and pushed on the bridge beam section. It moved enough for us to see a large metal hook that lay under it, along with an attached broken chain. I took pictures of it. This was good evidence that someone had removed the bridge. The question was why and why was it done secretively. That bridge went somewhere the night or early morning of the collapse.

"Look there, just on the other side of the beam, there is a loose rivet. Can you pick that up?" I asked.

"Yes, I can. Hold on." Arnold maneuvered the sub into just the right position and then he picked up the rivet with the mechanical arm.

"That's all I needed. Let's get out of here."

"You got it!" Arnold replied. Up we climbed. Approximately thirty feet from the surface something heavy hit the sub with a crash.

"Wow! What was that?" I asked.

"I don't know. Look it was a large rock! We are out in the middle of the river, so it did not just fall into the river. We are in danger," Arnold said.

"Can you take evasive action?"

"In this little thing? I will do my best. That was quite a shot for whoever did that. This is a relatively small target." Arnold said as he made the submarine zigzag through the water as we ascended. On the surface, we quickly opened the hatches. We saw a speedboat racing away. It was too far away to see any identification or see any faces. It was gone by the time I got my camera out.

"Oh, now would you look at that! There's a dent in the sub!" Arnold said. "If that big rock would have hit the sub just right we would be dead now."

"This case is getting more serious as well as more dangerous."

"Right, I think if there is nothing else, we need to get back to Erie as soon as possible."

"Fine with me, let's put that rivet in the truck and get out of here." I said.

We both hurried about our business of packing up. Soon, we were back on the road, north to Erie. It was not long before we noticed a large black car following us. Arnold was suspicious of it immediately. I was not sure what to think about it. Then, it closed the distance between it and the rear of the flatbed truck we were driving. Arnold slowed down, and at a place on the highway that widened, he waved the car around us. It was a black Lincoln similar to the armored one that American Presidents have been known to use. It slowly pulled around us. The windows were darkly tinted so that the interior was not visible. Just as it got in front of us, it slowed down. An unmarked tractor-trailer slammed up against the back of our truck.

"Whoa, these boys play rough!" Arnold exclaimed. He slowed the best he could and pulled off the road. The tractor-trailer passed by us barely missing the back of our truck. Once the truck came to a complete stop, we both got out of the truck and examined the rear of the truck to see if there was any damage done.

"You know that tractor-trailer wasn't even legal. It had no placards or even license plates, nothing! They tried to kill us I think." Arnold said.

"Maybe, it was just a warning. If they wanted to kill us, they would have." I replied.

"All this is over a bridge?"

"There must be more to it than what we may think," I said.

"Well, when we get to Erie, I'm done with it," Arnold said.

"Well, let's get going, then," I said, and we got back in the truck. Arnold did not waste any time getting there. He had a sigh of relief when we pulled into the marina to drop the sub off. He took the mini-sub off the flatbed truck with his lift that was made for such an operation.

"Here's your precious rivet," he said, taking it off the sub's mechanical arm. He placed it in a cardboard box and handed it to me. "Now, I have to fight with the insurance company to get this thing fixed, and re-inspected for safety. I did not expect death threats. That is a little too much for me."

After everything was squared away, we drove the truck back to his brother's lot.

"At least Alvin's truck isn't damaged in any way," Arnold said as we pulled in. Arnold went into the little shed that they had for an office and turned in the keys. We both got back in my car and I dropped him off at his marina.

"Be careful going back. That was just too close for comfort," he said as I pulled out.

"I know that is right. I will keep my eyes open, and you be careful also. They may not be through with either one of us." I said and left the parking lot.

The trip back to Clarion was without incident. I began to wonder if the problem I had on the road going to Erie was just a coincidence and not related to the case at all. I began wearing my 380 handgun, however, when I read in the newspaper two days later that Arnold had turned up missing. Now this was getting more than just interesting. There was more to this than just an old missing bridge involved. I realized that my fee that I was charging the Clarion Council should have been more than double of what it was.

5.

The Search for Witnesses and Photos

I REPORTED TO THE CITY Council the next day. I reported that I had made very little progress and had no further details than what they already had. They seemed a little disgruntled with that report, but I was unwilling to reveal to any of them any hard facts. I was and am always suspicious of everyone. I was not sure that someone on the Council was involved in this case more than anyone knew. So, I decided to keep their updates short and sweet.

The following day, I decided to look for people who may have been present that day. It would have been a big plus if I could come up with a photograph or two. I was pretty doubtful of having any success in this part of my investigation, since it had been tried before. I spent most of the day stopping in at local Main Street businesses and casually asking about what stores stay open late at night. It turned out that none of them did, except for one, a pharmacy. It had started an experimental policy of attempting a twenty-four hour, seven day a week service. That policy later failed, according to what I was told. The pharmacy now only stayed open until eight o'clock. It was a local shop, so I paid them a visit.

The pharmacist was new, so he was no source of information. The two clerks had been there less than three years so they could tell me nothing of value either. Then, I managed to get an interview with the owner in his office. It turned out, that he was there in the store the night in question. He was on late night duty that night since no one wanted to stay in the store all night and be bored. They had no customers after six that night, the best that the storeowner could remember. Then, I asked him about photos.

"Why yes, I do. I have a photo of a big truck that passed through here that night. It had a lead car with flashing lights and a trailing car with flashing lights. I could see inside the cars. There were several military men in uniform in each vehicle. I could not tell what branch of military it was. I did not recognize the uniform. It was very over-sized load, taking up both sides of Main Street. It tripped a couple of our power wires that go across the streets, and knocked out the traffic light on Fifth Avenue and Main. Those had to be repaired the next day."

"Wow, so did it have any identification on it?"

"No, absolutely none. It had no placards, and not even a license plate. The windows were darkened so that I could not even see the driver. It was really strange. I had never seen such a big truck pass through our town before. I had to run to the back and get my camera. It had already passed by the store when I got to the front with my camera. I had to run down the street to snap the picture. It must have had at least eighteen wheels under it. It was heavy duty that is for sure."

"Do you still have that picture?"

"I should still have it, yes. If you give me a minute, I will see if I can find it." He got up from his desk and went to his filing cabinet. He rambled through all the drawers and came up with nothing. Then, in the last file in the bottom drawer, he found it. "Hey, look at this! I found it!" He exclaimed and handed me the picture. It was notably foggy that night from the picture. He got a good picture of the rear of the truck that only displayed a large object covered with a tarp. Part of a front quarter panel of the trailing guard vehicle was visible in the lower right side of the picture. It load was very long and there were visible chains holding it down under the tarp. Not much of the cab could be seen due to the angle of the photo. The tractor itself was a Diamond

Reo, with conventional cab, C-114 model. I recognized it because my uncle once owned one a year or so ago. I considered the make of the truck to be a possible lead to ownership.

"This really doesn't show much, but then again, it shows a lot. May I borrow the picture for the investigation? I will return it."

"Well, I don't know. How about buying it, and then, you will not have to return it?"

"How much?"

"One hundred dollars."

"One hundred dollars for this three by five picture?"

"Take it or leave it. I will just put it back in the drawer. It can stay there. It must have some considerable value to you, so one hundred dollars, out the door."

"Great. Every time I turn around, it cost me money. Here's your hundred dollars." I handed him five twenty dollar bills.

"There you go. It's all yours," he said with a smile. He was still smiling when I left his office a hundred dollars poorer. I tucked the photo into my suit coat pocket, and walked down the street to the city park. The park was only once city block in size with two old, black cannons in the two corners facing Main Street and a tall statue in the center. There were four park benches facing Main Street and I noticed that the same elderly people often occupied them. They apparently came and sat on the benches just about all day, every day. So I decided to ask the ones present if they had seen the truck that had passed through town one night that took down some traffic lights.

I spoke to two bench occupants who were sitting together, and neither one of them claimed to know anything about a truck going through the town late one night. The third elderly man however did say he saw it.

"Yep, sure did. That was one monster load. They should have went around the town instead of through it, you know."

I wrote what he said down on my pocket note pad.

"What is your name, sir?"

"Lewis Zayzoff."

"Zayzoff? I never heard of it.

"I've been around for eighty one years, but if you don't come to the park much, you may have not ever heard of me."

"What were you doing on the park bench that late at night? From what I understand, it was around two or three in the morning that the truck passed through here."

"Couldn't sleep. I got up and came out here for some fresh air. I live in the apartment just above Murphey's Five and Dime. The one has a stovepipe stuck out the boarded up window. It's a short walk from there."

"Okay, what can you tell me about this truck?"

"There was a couple of fellers rid'n in a car in front of it, and a couple more behind it. They did not stop for nut'n. When the electrical wires got caught and snapped, they just kept on a truck'n."

"What kind of cars were they?"

"Both of em were Crown Vic's. Looked bran-new. Black, if I remember correctly."

"What about grey? Are you sure they weren't grey? Here look at this picture. In the corner of the photograph there is a partial front end of a vehicle. Is that one of them?"

The old man squinted his eyes and thought for a minute.

"Nope. That ain't one of em. These were Crown Vic's. They could have been police cars, but weren't. Them guys in the cars looked to be soldiers."

"Marines?"

"No, couldn't rightly say if they were soldiers for sure. They could have been some sort of militia, or foreigners."

"Foreigners?"

"Could have been, since I didn't recognize the uniform. The driver of the front car was squinty eyed, like he was Japanese, or Vietnamese, or some-thin."

"This gets stranger and stranger," I said.

"Anything else?"

"The rest might have been Russians for all I know. Nah, they just kept on going. Went that a way," he said and pointed to the direction of the Clarion River Hill.

"Has anyone else asked you about this?"

"Nah, no one. I've not told anyone else about it."

"Great. Keep it like that. Don't tell anyone that you have talked to me about it either, okay?"

"Sure, sure. It don't matter to me. I'll keep my mouth shut. Best that way."

I left him and walked to a different bench. There was another older man sitting there by himself.

"Hello, do you know anything about a big truck coming through here a few years ago, late at night? I knocked down some power lines."

"No sir, not a thing. I just moved here from Lancaster a couple months ago. Sorry, I can't help you," he replied politely.

I was satisfied with one eyewitness. It would have been better to have more, but one was better than none. Next, I went to my office and called West Penn Power, and asked them about any repairs that had to be done in Clarion back around March 31, 1969 or thereafter.

They put me on hold for a while, and someone besides the regular agent. I was put in touch with a next level supervisor.

"This is John Arnsworth. Who may we ask is calling?" the voice on the phone said.

"I am Inspector Zeb Dasher. I am doing an investigation concerning repairs done to the power lines and street lights in early April of 1969."

"Well, inspector you will have to get authorization from the Power Authorities in Harrisburg for that. I cannot just delve out that kind of information. You will have to contact their office, and they will send you a detailed report of any work done in that time frame."

"But do your records show any repairs done in and around that time on Main Street, Clarion?"

"Well, I can tell you that yes, there were some repairs done then, but I cannot give out any details concerning the matter. As I said, you will have to contact Harrisburg.

"Well, thank you, John," I said and hung up the phone. At least he acknowledged that something had happened back then, but he would not say what. I next followed through and called Harrisburg. They were nice and polite, and even promised me that they would send the requested information priority mail. I thought that to be unusual for a government agency to spend extra like that, just like that, but we would see if I get anything. I would have good information, hard evidence, when that envelope arrived. Things may be looking up.

The next day, I went in to give the city council my update. That only lasted three minutes, since I told them practically nothing. Several members seemed upset as I left. They would have to get over it, since I could not trust them with my information. I had the feeling that one or more of them knew all about what had happened that night, but no matter. My investigation went on.

6.

The Temptress

The next morning, I heard a knock on my office door. I do not have a fulltime secretary so I answered the door myself.

"Hello, my name is Sonita Elderidge. I represent the Clarion News Paper. You are familiar with our office on Main Street, are you not?" The young woman in a red, form fitting dress with a low cut neckline stepped in, uninvited.

"Well, why don't you come on in and have a seat," I said as I saw her sit down in the leather chair that faced my desk. "What can I help you with?"

"I am sort of on a fishing expedition. I was curious as to maybe you sharing a case or two with my readers. The news is rather dry right now; I need something to spruce my column up. Anything exciting or out of the ordinary that you could maybe share with me would be helpful." She said.

"Well, I don't know about sharing anything with you. All of my cases have legal attachments to them. I could have a lawsuit lowered on me if I divulged almost anything regarding any of my cases. Sorry."

"How about an old case? You surely have one that has been closed and dead for a while. How about one of those?"

"Oh, I may be able to give you something ancient, like when I was working in Pittsburgh or something. Most of those are long gone history."

"Great that is a start."

"Well, I have things to do, I can't just sit around here and tell you stories. I am involved in an investigation for the county. They expect results."

"That is just fine, Mr. Dasher. May I call you Zeb?"

"Zeb is okay. Mr. Dasher is a little formal, I guess."

" Good, you may call me Sonita. How about we get together after work and you can tell me about a case or two. Then, I will leave you alone. Sound okay?"

"Okay, that sounds like a date. If I am lucky, I will be able to quit today around five. I do not punch a time clock or anything but, I found that if I put in the time, I am rewarded with results. Often quitting time is around ten in the evening."

"Wow, you don't have a family?"

"No, my wife and I divorced over ten years ago down in Pittsburgh. She got the house, and the kids. I got the shaft,. The kids are all grown up now, so that is all over and done with."

"Oh, I see. I am single also. I have never been married. I have no children. Someday, I would like to settle down if the right man ever came along." She said and smiled. I then had the feeling that she was coming on to me. I was not sure I liked that. I was not really in the market for a new romance. My life was all business.

"How about we eat at Johnny Garneau's restaurant? It has good food." She said.

"Johnny's it is. I guess I should stop by and pick you up at your place." I said.

"Oh, that would be nice. I live on 286 South Fifth Avenue."

"Fifth Avenue? That's easy enough." I said. "How about seven o'clock? I need to get back home so I can get to bed fairly early. I have a busy day tomorrow. I think the only time I can give you now is at the restaurant."

"Well, that is a start. I will see you then."

Sonita left my office and I went back to work. I called my research friend at Penn. State and told him of my finding a bolt at the bottom of the Clarion River. I wanted to know if he could figure out where it came from. I needed to know what kind of machine it came off of and who made it. He agreed to look into it and he asked me to mail it to him. I agreed, so I boxed it up and mailed it to him by priority mail. He would get it the next day that way. I used his services before since he was quite good in his work. He would probably get back with me in less than a week, as he had on other occasions.

A little later that day, after lunch, I went to the news office and went through their files regarding the collapse of the bridge. There to my surprise I found a picture of the collapsed bride as it was half submerged in the water. I noticed in the picture that there was no sign of fog in the area. I took photocopies of the pictures and the news article with my instamatic camera. It produces a picture in sixty seconds. I did not see Sonita there in the newsroom, but I figured that she was probably out on assignment. This picture of the half-sunken bridge threw everything into a confusing mess. If this picture was true, then was this whole thing just a hoax of some sort?

I approached one person behind a desk there, "This picture," I said pointing to it still lying on the reading table. "This picture of the collapsed Clarion Bridge, who took it? Who was the photographer?"

"It had to have been Crag Crenshaw. He's our only photographer."

"Is he here? Can I talk with him?"

"He is only part time, like many of us. I think he did come in today. If he's here, he's in that room over there," the man at the desk said pointing to an open door on the other side of the room. I walked into the room and found a little, thin man of about fifty years of age tinkering with a thirty-five millimeter camera. I went over and sat down at the table where he was seated.

"Hello, are you Crag Crenshaw the photographer?"

"No, I'm Richard Nixon and this is a television set. Yes, yes, I am. How can I help you, sir?"

"The picture that is in the paper out on the reader's desk of the sunken River Bridge, did you take it?"

"Nope, sure didn't. That picture was sent in to us by mail, with no return address. I don't know who took it."

"Thank you sir, that is about all I needed to know." I said. After thanking the newsman at the front desk, I left. Back on Main Street, I decided to call my old police chief in Pittsburgh, Arnt Sigworth, and ask a favor. Back at the office, I called him. I sent him a copy of picture of the half-sunken bridge in the water that I had taken with my instamatic camera by way of my fax machine. He received it okay and wrote back that he would look into it, and get back with me. I sat back down at my desk, looked at my notebook, and jotted a few things down in it. Then, soon after I placed the little notebook back in my inner jacket pocket, the phone rang. It was my chief of police friend in Pittsburgh already with an answer.

"This picture you sent is a picture of a collapsed bridge in West Virginia. It collapsed back in fifty seven."

"So, that is not a picture of the Clarion River Bridge?"

"No, positive. I remember of that bridge in West Virginia collapsing. My grandmother lives down there."

"Wow that is very enlightening. Thank you, once again."

"Okay, Zeb, I hope you have a good progress in your investigation."

I hung up the phone and looked again at the photo from the newspaper. I did not see the natural spring fountain in the photo. It should have been visible. Also, there was no hint of fog anywhere, so that confirmed that it wasn't a picture of our bridge. I decided to call it quits for the day. I had many things to think about, and was not sure what I was going to do next. I put my jacket on, closed up my briefcase and went home. I shaved and took a shower when I got home. This Sonita was quite an attractive woman. She was about fifteen years my junior, which really did not bother me since she seemed to be mature for her age. I got along with her just fine, but really, in the back of my mind, I was not looking for romance or even a one night stand. It would just be nice to go out on a date for a change. I had not been on a date in decades, but I would not tell her that.

Seven o'clock rolled around soon enough, and I was hungry by then. I got in my car, and drove over to 286 South Fifth Avenue. She was already standing outside on the sidewalk waiting for me.

"Sorry, have you been waiting long?" I yelled out the open passenger window.

"Oh, no, I just came out here a second ago," she said and got in.

"Do I look okay?" she asked.

I looked over at her before putting my car back into gear. She wore a light blue, shiny looking dress that was again very low cut. I noticed that she was more than amply endowed. At least my one date in twenty years was good looking. I handed her a single red rose. She smiled and buckled her seat belt. We went on to the restaurant on route 322. The actual name of the restaurant was the Golden Spike. Since it was a smorgasbord, we were able to pick what we wanted to eat. Everything looked great, especially since I was starving by that time.

We sat down and began eating.

"So, how are you doing on your present case?"

"Oh, that case is still undecided. I have to sort out some facts. It seems like there is some misleading information floating about. I have to separate fact from fiction."

"Misleading information? Wow, so things aren't what they seem?"

"No, and it appears like there has been some sort of cover-up for unknown reasons. I don't know who is responsible for what yet, but I will get to the bottom of it."

"Are you good at getting to the bottom of things?" she asked with a devilish smile.

I did not answer but continued to eat. "Hey, your ribs are going to be cold if you don't eat them soon."

"I hope you don't mind me using my fingers. These things can be such a mess. I should have gotten something different, but they looked really good."

"They are really good. I've gotten them here before," I rapidly finished my plate. I ate much faster than she did. I was half way full and was going to require a second helping. I took off my jacket, and requested a new plate. The waitress brought a new plate to me and I went back to the smorgasbord. The mashed potatoes and gravy called my name this time, along with the freshly fried chicken. I filled my plate and sat back down.

"You certainly have a healthy appetite," Sonita said.

"Right, I should weigh three hundred pounds, but I'm barely over two hundred. I stay active, besides I work out on occasion."

"I like a man who knows how to take care of himself." She said and finished off the three ribs she had on her plate.

We finished our meals and I left a tip. Neither one of us wanted a dessert, so I took her home. I pulled up to the curb, and I got out and opened the car door for her.

"Sorry, I have to sort of eat and run, but maybe we can do this again real soon." I said as she got out of the car.

"Well, that sounds great," she said and handed to me a little slip of paper that had her phone number on it. "Thank you, I enjoyed the meal."

I closed the car door. She gave me a short, brief kiss on the side of my face and walked toward the large white house that had apartments in it.

She turned and said, "Call me!"

"Sure will. Maybe, in a few days we can do this again. I'll have to see how things work out." I said and got back in my car. I drove home thinking about this date. She certainly was tempting. It was the first in years, but would it be the last?

7.

Evidence Turns up Missing

The next morning, I got up and got dressed. I wanted to be at the office early. I went to my jacket to get my notebook and photo out of the inner pocket and found that it was not there. Then, I looked all over the bedroom for them, and found nothing. I went out to the car and found that there was nothing there either. I remembered of putting both in my jacket pocket, and I have never had anything ever fall out of it. So, I next went back to the restaurant to see if anything would turn up there. Just the manager and a prep-cook were there early in the morning. I was permitted to look around, and even check the trash. I came up empty handed. My thoughts turned to Sonita. Maybe she had seen them. She may even have them, so I called the number on the little piece of paper that she gave me. It was not a working number. I drove over to her apartment, and went to the little office just inside the front door. The woman behind the desk told me that there was no one by the name of Sonita Elderidge who lived there. Upset, I went to my office.

There I got on the phone with my friend at the state university.

"Oh, I'm glad you called. This bolt that you sent comes out of a crane manufactured by Wallace Crane in Malvern, Pennsylvania. Those bolts are special made for them."

"Great job! Is there anything else?"

"Yes, there is. If you want this thing back, you will have to come and pick it up yourself and take it back in this lead box. It is radioactive."

"What? Radioactive?"

"It looks like it has been exposed to very high grade uranium. I cannot send this thing through the mail, not even in the lead box. It is against the law."

"Okay, I'll be right over. It should take me about two hours to get there. Will that be okay?"

"Yes, it will be fine. I am a researcher. I am not heavily loaded down with a teaching schedule. I will be in my office until three this afternoon. I take a half an hour lunch break at twelve."

"Okay, I will be there shortly. Thank you. Do not let the bolt out of your sight. It's important." I said and hung up the phone. I got in my car and then took it to the gas station on the river hill. They had reasonable prices and service so I went there often. After that, I wasted no time getting to State College. I got on the newly constructed Interstate 80 east and then to route 220. With my foot resting heavily on the accelerator, I arrived there in record time. My research friend Dr. Richard Freemont was glad to see me.

"Zeb, how have you been?" he asked with an extended hand to me.

I shook his hand and said, "Well, I've been busy. I appreciate your assistance with things that I'm investigating."

"Right, any time, Zeb. So how did you come about getting this radioactive bolt?"

"I found it at the bottom of the Clarion River."

"Really, what a strange place for that."

"I thought so also. Well, where's it at?" I asked.

"Oh, it's right over there on that table. I would leave it in the lead box for your own safety. You may end up glowing at night if you don't."

"Just think I wouldn't need a flash light then, but yes, you are right. Safety is a top priority." I went over and lifted the lid to the box. The box was empty. "Richard, I thought that you said it was in this box."

"It is, or was," he replied and walked over to the box. "Oh my!"

"What happened?"

"I don't know. I place that in the lead box early this morning. I hadn't taken it out or even opened the box back up."

"Have you left the room or had visitors?"

"No, no visitors, but I did go to the restroom right down the hall about an hour ago."

"Did you lock the door when you left?"

"No, I never lock the door, except when I leave at night."

"People don't sign in to get on campus here, so there is no visitor record, unless they stop at the visitor's greeting office," Dr. Freemont said. He picked up the phone and called the visitor's desk and they reported no visitors signing in yet for the day.

"Whoa, that means someone has done some research on me and you. It also means that my phone has been tapped or my call was intercepted somehow." I said.

"Wow, I don't think any of that is legal," Richard said.

"No, it's not, and why does anyone want that bolt? What's the deal with it being radioactive?"

"It sounds like some deep espionage going on." My friend remarked.

"Okay, I'm out of here. Take care, my friend. Keep your eyes out for things or people that are unusual." I said while standing at the door, ready to leave. "Just be careful."

"I don't know if I like that warning."

"Do you carry a gun?"

"A gun? On campus? I should say not! I may be fired if I carried a gun on university property every day and the administration found out."

"Well, do you even have a gun?"

"I have a 30-30 rife that my dad gave me," Richard said.

"No, you need a personal defense weapon that you can carry with you at all times for protection," I replied.

"I think that is being paranoid."

"Not really. It is practical these days. Do you want to stay alive?"

"Of course I do, but I believe you are carrying this too far."

"I hope you are right, but get something, even if it's a little twenty-two. Something that goes bang may be all you need."

"Won't I need a license?"

"In this state, yes. Pay the fee, and get something that you can be comfortable carrying. Okay?"

"Well, I don't know."

"Promise me that you will, as a friend, a friend I want to keep around. I cannot be here to protect you, and the police are about worthless. They always arrive after the crime and then, it's too late."

"Well, if you insist."

"Okay, do it today."

"I'll get out of here a little early and take care of it. How's that?"

"Fine, just do it." I said and left for Clarion.

8.

People Turn Up Missing

The next day, I called Richard at State College and got no answer. I tried his home phone, and there was still no answer. I was not sure how to take that. He could be in a faculty meeting or in the classroom teaching, so I let it ride until the afternoon. That was a concern that I put on the back burner for now.

I called the Clarion News Paper to talk to the photographer, Crag Crenshaw, again about the phony photo of the bridge. I did not recognize the voice of the man who answered the phone. He told me that there was no Crag Crenshaw that worked for the newspaper. I put the phone down in shock. What was going on? I then remembered that my phone was probably tapped. I may not even be talking to the newspaper. I decided to walk the little ways down Main Street to the newspaper office. Once there, I walked in and saw a man that I did not recognize at the desk. Over the years, I had been in the newspaper office, and never seen this man before. I walked back to the photographer's room and it was empty. It did not even have desks, chairs or filing cabinets any longer. Amazed, I walked back out onto Main Street without saying a word.

Deep in thought, I walked across the street to the post office. I checked my mailbox and it had nothing in it. I noticed that I had not received anything from the power authorities in Harrisburg concerning repair expenditures. They said I would receive something by priority mail, but that never showed up. While on that side of the street, I walked down to the park, and saw that the park benches were empty. Usually, Louis Zayzoff was seated on the second bench, but today he was not to be found. I walked back down Main Street to Murphy's Five and Dime store and went up the stairs to the run down apartments above the store. I remember of him telling me that he lived in the room that had a stovepipe sticking out a boarded up window. That was the fourth window down from the stairway. Each room was small, so that meant it was four doors down. I knocked on the fourth door. There was no answer, so I tried the door handle. It had no lock, just a broken handle, so I pushed the door open. It glided open with a loud creaking sound. Inside I saw Louis Zayzoff lying on a twin-sized bed. He was dead. I went downstairs to the Murphy's store and used their phone to call the police. About ten minutes later Chief Shultzawich arrived. He asked me a few questions and then dismissed me from the scene. Later, I was informed that they considered Louis Zayzoff to have died of natural causes.

When I walked into my office on Main Street, I could tell someone had been in there. There were markings on the door that indicated that it had been forced open. What little evidence that I had, plus many of my files were gone. The notepad, the military pen and the old rotten military hat that I had found at the river site were gone. I called the police and they looked through the office, but reported nothing back to me. I was shocked to hear on the Clarion radio station later that day that the dead bodies of Arnold and Alvin Kribbs of Erie, PA. had washed up on the lake shore late yesterday afternoon. It was thought that they had been involved in a boating accident while fishing.

It turns out now that I had nothing, absolutely nothing. All my witnesses, and all the evidence were gone. Seriously disturbed now, I called my friend at State College and again was unable to get in touch with him. I called the dean of research there, and he told me that Richard had not showed up for his duties today, nor had he called. Now, I really had nothing to report to the city council! The news about Richard made me sick! I sat at my desk and considered what my next step should be. Whoever was involved with this bridge thing was deadly serious. This thing was beyond being a Mickey Mouse tourist attraction hoax. I pulled my 380 handgun from its concealed holster and checked the ammo. I loaded one shell into the chamber, and then replaced that one with another one into the magazine. Now all I had to do was pull the trigger, it was ready to fire. I went to my closet and pulled my bulletproof vest out. I took my shirt off and put the vest on. Then I put my shirt on over it. It made me somewhat uncomfortable, but it was better to be uncomfortable than dead. With all the evidence gone and all the witnesses gone, the only one left was me. So, I could be next on the hit list.

I was not sure what I was going to do next, perhaps it would be best if I left town for a while, for safety sake. I could continue my investigation even if I did not come to my office. I considered investigating the disappearances of my own evidence, but then, since the police were called in, it fell into their jurisdiction. Anything I done may be considered police interference. That accusation has never been pulled on me, but this case was so dirty, that I suspected it might go that way. I suspected that the police may not be one hundred percent on my side, but I had no proof of that. The city council and the police seemed to be legitimate, but I suspect everyone. Sorry that is just the way I am.

I then, made the decision to move my base of operations to a remote area, so I closed and locked the office door and went out to the car. After I got in, I turned the key and instead of starting, it only clicked. I got out and lifted the hood. There I was shocked to find a hot wire from the battery to a stick of dynamite and then to the starter. Apparently, the one who did the wiring did not secure large enough wires to carry the current. It only clicked the starter solenoid as a result of insufficient currency. Lucky for me it was messed up sabotage. I removed the dynamite and wires, so that I could leave. I did not bother with the police, since they seemed to never find anything. I did not doubt that there were no fingerprints to be found anyway. I fixed the wiring back to their original condition, and the car started right up. I drove home. I watched my rear view mirror for trailing cars. One car followed me at a distance and then turned off before I got home. I lived on Corbett Street, which was not very far from Main Street, so it only took a few minutes to get home.

Once home, I carefully opened the front door with my gun drawn. I cautiously went in and got my things. Soon, I was out of there carrying my bare essentials. I decided to go southeast to my grandfather's old farm. It was located some miles out of town in a deep valley surrounded by tall, virgin timber. It was a secluded place, and I felt that I would be safer there than at my home on Corbett Street or at the office. It was about a half hour's drive to get there, along some curvy, Pennsylvania roads.

Once I got there, it was a long drive down into the valley by way of a rocky, dirt driveway. A person really needed a four-wheel drive vehicle to go up and down that driveway, especially in the wintertime. I did not have a four-wheel drive vehicle, but I had learned how to navigate the sharp pointed boulders that stuck up in the driveway. If a person was not careful, they could get their car stuck on those big rocks, or else have the undercarriage of their car ruined by them.

The old farmhouse was a welcome site. It has an old wood frame. Two story house that had been built back in the eighteen hundreds. There were all sorts of ancient antiques located throughout the property like old plows, pitchforks, milk churners and the like. Upstairs was great grandpa's old shotgun that dated back to the late eighteen hundreds. There was not much furniture either, a stove, an old refrigerator, kitchen table and chairs, one living room chair and a bed upstairs. It had no modern conveniences like hot and cold running water. The kitchen sink had a pump that had to be worked manually. There were no other houses or farmhouses anywhere near this place, so I was comfortable that I was alone. Farm Valley stretched for miles so this place was not the only farm in the area. These farms were spread far apart due to the acreage of the crop fields.

I took all my things into the house from the car and settled in for the day. I would skip going to the office for a while and concentrate on doing mobile investigations. Sadly, the old farmhouse had no telephone, so I was at a standstill in many ways. Maybe, I needed a day off or two anyways. I would be safer that way. If my evidence and my witnesses all disappeared, then, there was a strong probability that I would be next. I wore my bulletproof vest quite often, now, and walked around with my small handgun tucked into my pants. Even at the old farm, I was not comfortable. Occasionally, I would peek out a window. Once or twice, I went outside and walked around the front yard area, but came back in quickly, suspecting someone could shoot me with a high power rifle. Yes, I was quite paranoid at the time, but I had good reason to be.

9

Threats

Monday morning, I went to the office to continue my investigations. It seemed like a waste of time, now, that all my evidence and all my witnesses were gone. I was at a standstill weeks into my investigation. I now had nothing, so I was not happy. I decided to call State College to find out about my friend, Richard. I talked to the dean and he told me that Richard was dead. His body was found face down in a gutter just outside of town. It was now a homicide case. The police wanted to talk to me about it. Actually, I did not know anything about his murder since I was not there, and I had no names. What could I tell them? I could tell them actually, nothing. I called the police department there and told them such, but they wanted a signed statement to that effect. I just hung up since it was not helpful. I would probably hear from them again, later.

As soon as I hung up the phone, it rang.

"Hello, Zeb Dasher's Detective Agency, may I help you?"

There was silence on the other end of the line.

"Hello, if you are not going to answer, why waste my time?" I hung up the phone, and it rang again. "Hello, Zeb Dasher's Detective Agency, may I help you?" Again, nothing. I hung up, and it rang again.

I picked up the phone and said nothing this time. I could hear someone breathing on the other end of the line. Then, a silent chuckle could be heard before the phone went dead. My phone was now out of order. I stepped out of the front door on to Main Street; suddenly I heard a whizzing sound just over my head. A bullet hole appeared on the doorsill. Then I heard the crack of a gun, so I pulled my gun out and stepped back inside the office. I could not call out for help, so I decided to see if I could go out the back door of the building. The back door emptied into a small nameless alley that ran parallel to Main Street. Main Street stores to receive shipping used it. I cautiously walked outside, gun drawn, and looking around. I walked the length of the alley to the police station by the County Court House, and went in. There I met a sergeant at the front desk.

"Zeb Dasher! What brings you our way?" Sergeant Meir asked. I had talked with him several times over the years and he seemed like a competent man.

"Someone just took a shot at me when I came out of my office."

"A shot? Here in town? Did you see who it was?"

"No, but it came from the Public Library area."

The sergeant went back to the captain's room and came out shortly.

"Get in the police car, let's go down and take a look." We went out and got in the police car that was parked besides the building. "Do you have any idea of who would want to do something like that?" He asked as we pulled out.

"No, I literally have no clue, sergeant. I had been working on the missing bridge case, so maybe it's somehow related to it."

"The missing bridge case? That case has been moth-balled a few years back." He said as we went down Main Street.

"Right, but the city council want answers about it and have hired me to find them.'

"Well, I'm not sure why, but okay. To me, that is just water under the bridge, so to speak. It is a dead letter issue with the police department. So, just why would someone be shooting at you concerning a bridge that has been missing for years?"

"I wish I knew," I said as we parked in front of the Clarion Public Library.

We both got out and started looking around. We walked around the post office, the around the library and then the antiques house at the corner.

"If someone was shooting at you from here, it was a long shot," Sergeant Meir said. "From here, you can see most of Main Street, but with traffic and all, it would be a pretty good shot."

"He missed, remember."

"Maybe, he missed on purpose. You don't know."

"You mean a warning shot? I really doubt it. I think he or whoever it is, plays for keeps."

"Here we go," the sergeant said as he picked up a spent shell on the ground. He put it to his nose, "This thing has just been fired," he said. He handed the shell to me to look at.

"A thirty ought six hunting rifle." I reported.

"Well, that would do it. If they wanted you dead, one of those would do the job."

"Someone took out my office phone service before this happened. They tried harassing me with phone calls first."

"Let's take a look at your phone lines," Meir said.

We walked down the street to my office. The officer walked around the building and found that the phone lines had been cut that were going into my office.

"I've seen enough. Let's go back to the police station and we will see if we can get the phone company to tell us who called you, and from where."

We rode back to the police station and went inside. The sergeant got on the phone with Bell Telephone. He had to get management approval for such a request, but they seemed cooperative. Soon he had the information that he needed.

"The phone calls all came from a Mr. Haddoc on Second Street. Let's go," he said. We both got back into the police car and went to the address on Second Street. It was a street that had a lot of old two and three story houses built back in the early nineteen hundreds. We stopped at a large, white three-story house that had no porches. We got out of the police car, and went to the front door. The sergeant knocked on the front door. We waited. He then banged on the front door. A little old woman came to the door.

"Yes sir. May I help you?" she said in almost a whisper.

"I'm looking for a Mr. Haddoc. Does he live here?"

"Mr. Haddoc?" She asked and just stood there as if she did not understand the question. I suspected that she had dementia.

"Is there a Mr. Haddoc living here?"

"Well..."

"May, we take a look around?"

"I suppose..."

We pushed on by her and into a large hall. A grand staircase went up three floors. We went and knocked on all the bedroom doors, and there was no one in any of them. After coming to the last door on the third floor, we decided to check the attic. There was narrow stairways that lead to the attic. The sergeant drew his gun out and had it ready when we got to the top of the stairs. He opened the door and went in. I followed closely behind him. There was a bed and some clothing on the floor, and an open window. We looked around the room and there were no papers and only a few clothes. The sergeant went to the window and looked out.

"Hey, Dasher, come look at this."

I went over and looked down. Below, on the grass lay the body of Mr. Haddoc.

"Do you suppose we found our man?"

"Maybe." I replied.

It turned out that it was not a dead Mr. Haddoc at all but a James Ridshaw. The coroner made the positive identification from the man's fingerprints. He was a former navy officer and ex-CIA man who had been relieved of his duties because of questionable dealings with the Soviet Union. Apparently, he was expendable.

Back at the police station, Sergeant Meir gathered information of Mr. Haddoc. It turned out that he was associated with the Defense Department and the Department of Justice. He had worked for the Defense Department for over ten years and then sidelined with various missions overseas for the Department of Justice tracking down international criminals. There was no phone found in the Second Street apartment that was associated with Mr. Haddoc, yet Bell Telephone stated that the call was indeed made from there by a phone line paid for by Mr. Haddoc. The old woman who answered the door proved to be of no help to the police.

At the end of the day, I drove back to my secluded farmhouse out in the woods. I was careful to watch for possible cars following me. It would do no good as a hiding place if it had become known where it was. The sergeant told me to stay in hiding. I stopped and bought some groceries on the way to the farmhouse and some clothing. I had no idea how long I would have to hide.

10.

Hiding

I put up the groceries on the old dusty shelves when I got back to the farmhouse. The whole house needed cleaning. The outside of the house had not been painted in decades. There was not even a hint of paint on the outside woodwork. The house used to be white while granddad lived there, but no one ever tended to it after he died. The barn was in disrepair also. I parked my car inside the barn. The tin roof of the barn was heavily rusted but did not leak. There was still hay in the lofts from where we had horses to plow the fields. Granddad had worked those fields over the years and had produced a lot of corn, cabbage and tomatoes. I could almost see him out there in the field even now, plowing behind his two horses.

In the evening, it was always very quiet down in the farm valley. There was not even the slightest hint of any highway traffic sound or city noise. Only crickets and an occasional bird or owl sounded off in the evening. It was actually nice to relax here. I had thoughts of retiring to this very spot someday if all went well. I just had to pay the property tax and maintain the upkeep. That was okay, and it really did not amount to much. I just hoped that I would survive long enough to retire. The present case sort of threw doubts on that prospect.

When the sun went down if was very dark in the valley. The only light there was come from the moon. I walked out on the front porch and took in a deep breath. All the trees and tall grass in the fields had filtered pure and fresh air. I looked out into the fields and watched the tall grass blow in the slight breeze. It certainly was as peaceful as it was dark there. Then, I became suspicious of the shadows. A tree on the other side of the field in front of the house had one too many shadows. I could not tell if it was another small tree just behind it or if it was a man stooped down there. I was not sure, so I went back inside the house. Maybe, I was suffering from paranoia. It was not good to worry, especially if it was nothing. Since the house had no electricity, I had to walk around with an antique lantern. There were candles in the house, also, but they did not produce as much light as the lantern. There were several lanterns in the house, one for every room actually. Most of them still had kerosene in them that still burned. I liked the lanterns because I could easily adjust the amount of light that it put out by turning a little metal knob under the globe. I decided to go upstairs to go to bed, but if there was someone outside watching, I did not want to telegraph my movements. I put out the light.

While standing in the dark, I looked out the front room window. Out into the fields, I searched for movement. There appeared to be nothing at first. I did not see the shadow by that tree any longer. That fact bothered me. Where did it go? I sat my lantern down, went into the kitchen, and looked out the window that was over the sink. I could see the barn and the driveway that went up the steep hill. After studying that scene for a while, I saw nothing moving. Then, I went and checked the front door dead bolt, it was secure. I went back to the large living room and checked the back door's dead bolt. It was secure also. The bottom floor only had three rooms in it: the kitchen, the front room and the back living room. The front room had a closet in it as if it could have been used as a bedroom at one time. The stairway to the second floor went up in the front room. I went and carefully looked out the back window. There was a good view of the backfield that went all the way to the creek. There were not trees in that field, but there were some around the creek. I watched there for movement, and saw none.

I decided to just go upstairs. With the lantern turned out, it was a situation where I had to feel my way up the steps. I lay down in the bed at the top of the stairs. I could see out the window, but there was really nothing to see. I kicked my shoes off and put my handgun under my pillow. I was tired so I was off to sleep soon. Around two in the morning, some flashing lights coming from the sky awakened me. I took my gun out from under the pillow and went over to the window.

High in the sky I could see some sort of flying craft. It could have been a helicopter, but it did not hear the familiar chop-chop sound that a helicopter makes. This thing was silent. Suddenly, a bright light shone out of the very bottom of the craft. It was extremely bright and it lit up the entire farmhouse. I stepped back away from the window. I am not sure, but this thing was probably some sort of surveillance vehicle. I had my car parked in the barn so that it was not visible from the air. This thing hovered quietly above the house for several minutes. I did not move from my spot until it left. I looked out the window when the bright light went out. The thing in the sky was gone. I was unfamiliar with the craft. Next, I wondered what such a strange machine was doing in farm valley. There was nothing but farms in this valley, so there was nothing out of the ordinary to spy on. The only thing that I could conclude was that they were looking for me. Of course, the big question that remained was, who was "they?"

I put my shoes back on and my bulletproof vest. Grabbing great granddad's old double-barreled shotgun, I went carefully downstairs. It was really dark, so I had to take my time and feel my way down the steps. Carefully, I made my way to the front window. I looked out at the front field. There was no movement, so I made my way to the front door and opened it slowly. Sticking just my head out of the front door, I looked around. It was quiet and I saw no movement. I stepped out onto the front porch and looked across the front field. The far tree had no second shadow. I crouched down and made my way out to the edge of the field. I sat down in the tall grass and waited. I sat there for at least ten minutes. I was wide-awake, so I was not in any hurry to go back to bed. Suddenly, I saw movement in the field close to the suspected tree. It was a deer.

Next, I slowly made my way around to the back of the house, using the tall grass as a cover. I could see nothing unusual there, so I made my way back to the front porch. Just as I was going inside, I heard something. It sounded like someone was slowly walking, but I could not quite tell from what direction the sound was coming. At first, I thought it was perhaps the deer that I had just seen, but that animal had disappeared into the woods. This was a deliberate, slow pace. I crouched my way to the corner of the house and surveyed the driveway area. Past the barn, and halfway up the hill, in the dark shadows, I could detect movement.

I pulled the hammers back on both barrels of the shotgun and waited. I had my handgun as backup. Whatever it was, it was coming closer. Then, whatever was in the darkness, seemed to split. Now I could hear two paths being made. Slowly, ever so slowly, it came closer. My finger was on both triggers. Then, I heard a twig snap in the field behind me. I swung around and studied the dark field. Again, I detected no visual movement, yet I could hear something.

Turning back around, facing the driveway up the steep hill, I could see someone or something now in the shadows on both sides of the driveway. My flashlight was still in the car. It was not too bright to have left it there, but I did not anticipate this. Whatever or whoever it was, still lurked in the darkness. Again, something behind me moved. I turned and looked, yet nothing. At that moment, whatever was coming down the hill toward me, was now rushing forward while my back was turned. I swung around and pulled both triggers. The big blast of pellets would surely hit something. I could hear something or someone groan. All movement stopped. Whatever had been approaching from behind me was now rapidly going in the opposite direction. I stood up and hurried back into the farmhouse. Bolting the door behind me, I went back upstairs to look out the upstairs windows. Even though the view was better, I still saw nothing unusual. I stayed up until four thirty, and then went back to bed. It had been a long night.

The next morning, it was bright and sunny. I went outside and walked around with my handgun in my belt. I went up the hill part way and examined both sides of the driveway. There was blood found on a clump of grass. Whatever, or whoever was hiding in the darkness last night, stayed in the grass and left no footprint. I assumed it was a deer that was hit last night, but I was not sure.

11.

Undercover Cloak and Dagger Stuff

I pulled the blood-covered grass and put it in an envelope. I was going to give it to Sergeant Meir to have analyzed. I needed to know if it was animal or human blood. In addition, as a precaution, I went to the barn and jump-started grandpa's old 1951 Chevrolet car. I had been starting it and driving it down the road a short distance just about each time that I came to the farm to keep it operational. It started up right away and ran quiet. It had an in line six cylinder in it with a three speed stick shift on the column. I left it run while I got ready to go into town.

I intended to drive it to town and turn in the blood sample to the sergeant as soon as I got my disguise on. I have worn disguises before of rare occasions. This time I felt it was a necessary precaution. I put my bulletproof vest on under the old woman's dress that I was going to wear. I wanted to look like an old grandmother who came into town for groceries, but I would stop at the police station first. Next, I put a white haired wig on and then a scarf over that to hold it in place. I wore a long, one-piece dress that went almost to my knees. Looking in the old mirror hanging on grandpa's bedroom wall, the disguise seemed to be convincing enough.

I got into the old car and babied it up the steep driveway. Out on the road, it wanted to sputter at first, but that smoothed out after a while. Once in town, I stopped at the police station that was beside the courthouse. It also served as a jail. When I got out of the car, I had to shift my clothing around some. Since I was not built like a woman, the outfit really did not fit me all that well. I went in and stopped at the front desk. The sergeant was there as usual.

"Yes, may I help you, Madame?" he asked.

"Great, you didn't recognize me. Would you have the coroner's office analyze this sample of blood to see if it's human or animal, please." I handed him the envelop. He looked in it at the bloody grass.

"Dasher? Good disguise. Hmmn, where did you get this?"

"At my hideout. How soon do you think I can get the results?" I asked.

"I'll send it over to the coroner's office right now. He will let me know shortly," the sergeant said. "Rick! Get over here. I need you to run this down to the coroner's office. We need to know if it's human blood on that grass or animal blood."

A young officer who had his left arm in a sling and his upper arm bandaged got up from his desk and received the envelope from Sergeant Meir.

"What happened to him?" I asked.

"Fell out of a tree and broke his upper arm." Meir replied.

The young man quickly went out the front door without a word.

"Should I wait here? How long do you think it will be?" I asked.

"I don't know. It depends on how busy the coroner is at the time. I'd say, come back around two."

"Okay, I'll be in my office until then. I'll be back at two." I left and drove the old car down the back alley to the back door of my office. As soon as I opened the back door, and before I could turn the light on, I saw a flash of light and then heard a loud bang! I was struck squarely in the chest with a bullet. Whoever it was went out the front door in a hurry. I was stunned by the bullet's impact. I hurried to the front door as fast I could go. I slung the front door open, and saw no one running down the street. I walked out onto the sidewalk and looked up and down Main Street, I did not see anyone to pursue. I looked at my dress, and now it had a good-sized hole in the very front of it. It was not reusable.

I examined the front door lock and concluded that it had been forced open. I went to my supply closet, got my dusting equipment out, and then, dusted for prints. There were none, so obviously, the intruder wore gloves. After that, I called State College and inquired about the homicide case concerning my research friend. The dean asked me whom I was talking about. I repeated his name, and the dean said that no such person was a faculty member, and according to his record, there never was such a person who taught there by that name. I was shocked, but perhaps at this point, not surprised. I thanked him and hung up. How in the world does such a thing as this happen? I did not know the dean personally, but what happened? My friend had just been erased. It seemed like I was slated to be erased also. I had a few tricks up my sleeve to prevent that from happening. Actually, this was a bewildering case that I hoped I would survive.

Next, I called the police department, and talked to Sergeant Meir. He told me that the blood had been analyzed and it turned out to be animal blood. I thanked him for the information and quick service. I felt like he was a good man, but when I sat down at my desk to think things out, I was inclined to change my mind. I suspected that the sergeant was lying. I did not have any idea why he would lie, but in my line of work, I live by my suspicions. This time, maybe my suspicions would keep me alive.

I contemplated notifying the FBI concerning this case. It appeared to be beyond the scope of my investigative abilities since all my evidence and witnesses were gone. Now, my life was in danger. I needed help, and I just was not sure the local police was able to do much for me. I decided to go ahead and call the FBI office in Pittsburgh. I had dealt with them before with some success.

"FBI, how may I direct your call?"

"This is detective Zeb Dasher; I need to talk with an agent, please"

"What may I ask is the reason for the call?"

"I'm dealing with several cases of missing persons, and murders. I need a little assistance, please."

"Thank you, Mr. Dasher. I will get the next available agent to help you. Please hold...."

I waited on hold for a good ten minutes, and then and man's voice began speaking to me.

"Mr. Dasher?"

"Yes sir, who am I speaking with?"

"Special Agent Riley, tell me why you are calling sir."

"I have witnessed the disappearance of my research specialist at State College. In addition, I have had several people around me murdered. All my evidence on a case that I am working on has been stolen. I have reason to believe that my life is in danger, also."

On such matters as what you are describing, we refer the caller to the local authorities. Have you done that?"

"Yes, I am working with the local police, but getting nowhere."

"Patience, Mr. Dasher, patience. Investigations take time. You may ask for police protection from the local police if you feel threatened."

"It is more than a feeling, I was just shot at. Fortunately, I had my vest on under my clothes."

"Great, it is a good idea to keep wearing that for as long as you are investigating the missing bridge case. So, let the police know your concerns, and if anything, get back in touch with us. Thank You."

"Wait, how did you know I was investigating the missing bridge?"

The FBI hung up. So, the FBI was aware of my investigations? Who told them? Surely not the local police. Maybe someone on the city council had talked to them. I was not sure. I decided to just go back to the farmhouse for the rest of the day. I had a lot to think about. I was not sure what I was going to do next. I was at a standstill in the investigation. I considered reporting in to the city council and asking them to relieve me of the case. I had never done that with any case. Such a move may ruin my reputation, but then, what good is my reputation if I am dead.

I made sure my disguise was in place and gun ready before I stepped out the back door. I slung the door open and waited. Nothing happened, so I got into my car and drove back toward Farm Valley. On the way back, a black Lincoln came up close to my back bumper. There was no way to out run that behemoth in my old gallop so I slowed down. A slower pace would permit the car to go past me. Instead of passing me, the black car behind me tried pushing me. My old car was heavy, probably heavier than any newer car, so it did not push very easily. After the first push, I slowed down to a crawl. We came to a sharp curve in the road, and at that moment, the car from behind accelerated. It slammed into my car's back bumper, throwing my old car out of control. My car careened off the road, and down a slight hill. I slammed on the brakes and brought it to a quick halt. I got out of the car and inspected it for damage. The car was still running, and everything looked functional, so I babied it back up the hill and on to the road. The black Lincoln was gone, but not forgotten.

I was glad to see the old farmhouse again. It was a welcome sight. I felt safer here than in town, but after last night, I knew I still had to be on my guard. I pulled the car into the barn and got out. I got rid of the wig on the way in. It made my head sweat. I unlocked the front door and opened it. It appeared that no one was inside so I cautiously entered. After checking out the place, I sat down at the kitchen table to relax and think. What a day this had been!

12.

Attempted Assassination

Therefore, the best I could tell, this whole thing about the bridge was much more involved than I originally knew. The case was proving to be a big one. After talking with the FBI in Pittsburgh, I suspected that they were involved in the whole affair somehow. I decided that tomorrow, back at the office, I would call my police friend in Pittsburgh. He had been helpful before, and he would probably prove to be helpful again. I did not have very many friends left. The ones that I did have, and were not involved in the case, I stayed away from. I did not want to put any of them in danger. On second thoughts, maybe I should use a different phone than the one at the office. I could use one of my friend's phones, but I dared not to go around anyone that I cared about.

Next, I decided that I would use the office phone only for giving false information and misdirection to whoever was tapping in on my conversations. I considered that one of my better ideas. I could set up a sting operation of my own. This could bring out the real culprits into the open. Next, I had to figure out who on the police force was on my side and had not been compromised. I suspected Meir but I had no evidence. I was used to not having any evidence in this case.

I needed to leave hints of bait for the sergeant to see if he bit on it. That certainly would clear some things up. If the sergeant was compromised, then, how far up the latter did the compromise go? The police chief seemed legitimate to me, but then so did Meir at first.

I got some sandwich meat out of the refrigerator and took two slices of bread out of the bread bag resting on the kitchen sink. A little mayo and a little mustard, and poof, I had a sandwich. It was going to take more than just one sandwich to keep me from feeling hungry, so I made another. After that, I went back to the sink and washed up some for bed. I usually can do some clear thinking before I go to sleep. Sometimes I do my best thinking before sleeping, which seems to be opposite of most people. Sleepy heads are not thinking heads but I turn things repeatedly in my mind before getting sleepy. I use the mental exercise to wear my mind out for the night. There are times that I dream about a case.

I got into my pajamas and lay down on my bed. What kind of bait did I need? I then realized that I did not need real bait. As long as they thought, I had something that may be enough to draw whomever into my net. I would have to make something up. It could be something that I suspected to be real. Yes, but what? I set my mind to thinking about the entire case. Maybe, I can propose that I have the hook that was down at the bottom of the river. I can hint that I have it somewhere, somewhere in my office. Let us see who shows up for that.

It was dark by the time I came up with that idea, and I turned my lamp off to go to sleep. I was worn out both mentally and physically by the time midnight rolled around. I fell asleep shortly after that, but was awakened by a loud creaking sound coming from the stairway. I pulled my gun out from under my pillow, and slowly got out of bed. I knelt behind the chest of drawers on the other side of my bed. I could faintly detect footsteps at the top of the stairs. Slowly, ever so slowly the person became visible in the faint light.

Suddenly, there was a stream of fire spewing out of a machinegun. It lay waste my bed where I had been sleeping just a few minutes before. It stopped and the intruder stood there motionless looking at the empty bed. Hiding in the darkness behind the chest of drawers, I took aim and fired one shot. The intruder dropped to the floor. I stood back up and waited. The dark figure on the floor was motionless. I waited a little longer to see if he had a backup companion. No one appeared, so I lit my lantern and walked over to the man lying on the floor. He wore a dark mask. His left arm was in a sling. I did not need to remove the mask to know who it was. I dimmed the lamp down and sat it down on the floor by the dead man. I walked over to the stairway and looked down. I could not see anyone, but it was dark at the bottom of the stairs. I went back over to my closet and put on my vest over my pajamas. Slowly, I descended down to the bottom of the stairs. I stood there in silence for a few minutes to see if I detected any movement. The front door was open. I walked over to the open door and looked out. All I could hear was crickets.

Suddenly there was a very bright light coming down from a flying craft above the house. It hovered silently just above the roof of the house. I could not tell just what the craft looked like because the light shining on the house was blinding.

Then, I heard a strange noise that came in strong pulses. I closed the front door to keep the pulses out, and then just as suddenly as they had started, they stopped. I opened the front door slightly and looked out. The pulses had flattened the tall grass nearby. Whatever it was in the sky, it circled the house several times before quickly disappearing into the dark clouds of the night.

I determined then, that I was going to get my hunting rifle from my home on Corbett Street and see if I could bring that thing down if it ever came that close again. I may at least put the light out so I can get a good look at what it was that was flying overhead. My going back to my home in town may not be a wise decision, so I decided instead to leave now and go to my Cousin Bruce's house in Greenville, PA. He was an avid hunting enthusiast and had many different rifles and ammo. He was the right choice. I always got along with him just fine, so I decided to leave now while it was dark. I would not stay there long for his safety sake. I would just stay long enough to borrow a hunting rifle. We had been hunting together for years and had shared rifles before. He had a nice collection. If I left now, I would be there at daybreak. I would not stay, even though I knew that they would insist on my staying for breakfast. I quickly got dressed, and put a few essentials in my car. I took the flashlight out of the glove box and looked under the hood. Everything looked fine, so I started the car. I ran back in the house, got a few more things, and then drove to the top of the hill. The highways were deserted this early in the morning. I decided to drive the interstate most of the way, and then get off onto small side roads. It was the fastest and easiest way to get there.

I arrived at Bruce's doorstep at seven o'clock that morning. His family is early a riser so seven o'clock was not very early for them. After a warm greeting, I explained my situation. They all showed deep concern for my safety. I was welcome to stay at their house for as long I wanted, but I did not dare put them in danger. I had survived the night. I wondered what the day would bring. Under the circumstances, Bruce let me have his high-powered moose rifle and a box of shells. He said it would bring down a rhino. I was impressed with the weapon. I bid them good-bye and decided to not go back to Clarion, due to the now dead body of one of their police officers. I was sure they had probably located the dead body by now. I listened to the radio in the car as I drove across the state line into Ohio. Yes, I was wanted for questioning concerning the death of a local police officer. It was not listed as a homicide yet, but it was under investigation. There was no mention of the machinegun that was in the hands of the dead police officer. There was no mention of how my bed was sprayed with bullets. So, why were the police trying to kill me, or maybe it was just one or two of them. I was not sure of many things. I was sure that I needed to stay out of sight for a while.

I stopped in Youngstown, Ohio where another one of my cousins lived. He lived well off the beaten path, and was considered by some in the family as rather anti-social. I knew him pretty well being that we went to the same high school together. He had served in the military Special Forces in Vietnam. He came home as a decorated hero, but rather recluse. He had inherited a fortune from his father, and did not work any job since Vietnam. I drove down his long, rough driveway and stopped at his barrier. There was a big pipe set across width of the driveway that I could not get around. I got out of the car and walked the rest of the way to his camouflaged cabin that was located on the side of a hill.

He was standing there in front of the cabin door by the time I got to the small porch.

"Rick! What is going on, man? How have you been?" I said

"Zeb, good to see you. I have been keeping my head down, staying out of the man's way. You know you cannot trust anyone. They killed the Kennedys, you know. They took out Nixon because he was an anti-communist. He knew about them and was going to spill the beans."

"Well, you haven't changed a bit. I think I understand now a little what you mean about the corruption in government, though. With recent events, I guess I'm beginning to see the light."

"Events? What kind of events are you talking about?" Rick asked. He always viewed himself as being well informed. Now, I seriously wondered just how much truth was in what he had told me in the past. Maybe it was more true than what I had previously realized. Some of the things he held on to just could not be true, as if the communists had secretly taken over the country, and that we had only their political flunkies running things in DC now. We sat down on the two chairs on the front porch and I told him about my missing bridge case. I listened intently. After I told him the last detail, he was silent and somber.

"Let me think on that some. Come on, let us go in and get something to eat. Are you hungry?"

"Starved."

13.

Secret CIA Files

After we ate, we sat in his little living room and talked. He seemed to hint that he would be able to help me. I also hinted back that I would appreciate any help that I could get.

"Listen, Zeb. I have an inside man at the CIA, who is a friendly. I will get in touch with him. He has helped me before on some serious stuff. So, I recommend that you stay here. We will see what we can come up with in a day or two. I would not worry about your being a suspect back in Pennsylvania. We are going to arrange it so you show up dead. From here on out, you will drop out of sight. I have a man in Arlington that can arrange a fake death, body and all, for anyone in the continental U.S. After that, you will need a new ID, so we can maneuver without being tracked and hunted. From what it sounds like to me, the CIA is deeply involved in the bridge case."

"I believe so. There are a lot of questions that need answers."

"So, are you with me, then, Zeb?"

"Yes, I certainly am."

"Good. We will get started with it in the morning. There is a lot to be done, so we will get a fresh start tomorrow. Right now, I have to go and tend to the generator in the shed. I do not have electrical lines out here, so I generate my own electricity. I also grow my own food. We are having a salad later."

"That sounds good, Rick."

"It will be. Next, I need to tell you that the bathroom is out back. I do not have a regular phone. I have a portable phone with batteries in it. It is an encrypted phone because I only talk to a few people that I trust."

He walked over to a table and picked up a large, oversized looking phone receiver that was not attached to a base.

"See, here it is," he said holding the phone up.

"Wow, is all this necessary?"

"Sorry to say yes, but it is. You see I have done some serious international missions right after Vietnam, and I need to be as secretive as possible. There are things that I've done that no one ever needs to know about."

"So, your life is in danger also?"

"No, probably not, at least not immediately like you. There are probably foreign agents still out there who would like to see me disappear, but it would be a challenge for them." He smiled.

"Wow, I had no idea. I just thought that you were rather antisocial."

"That too. Here, I'm going to call my CIA man, and see if I can get things rolling." He picked up the phone and walked into a back room to talk in private. I had never seen a phone as he had, but I have heard of car phones. This was sort of like one of those.

About a half an hour later, Rick came out of the back room with a smile on his face. "It's all set. We will ride to DC tomorrow to see my man down there. The Arlington man also said that he would get things going for you, complete with new identification. You will be a new man after tomorrow, my friend."

"So, we will just go down there and things will be okay then?"

"Well, hopefully everything turns out okay. There are always snags in the weave of life. Now, if you will excuse me, I am going out back and check on the generator. It has one big supply tank that has to be drained into a smaller tank that is attached to the generator to eliminated moisture. It will run about a day and a half on the one small tank. It is about due for a refill. I'll be right back." Rick said and went outside. He came back about ten minutes later. "All done," he said and then sat back down on his easy chair.

We sat and talked for the rest of the evening and went to bed at nine o'clock that evening. I slept on the sofa in the front room. He slept in the one bedroom. I noticed that he did not lock his door before going to bed. He told me that it was not necessary. He had his own security system. He said, "Locks only kept the honest people out, don't you know?" He closed his door to the bedroom and I stretched out on the sofa. I had one big pillow, which really proved to be too big for the sofa. It kept falling off onto the floor throughout the night.

Early in the morning, close to three-thirty the lights in the house all came on and turned off repeatedly. Rick came rushing out and flipped a switch next to the front door that turned all the lights off

"Shhh, there's someone or something out there..." he whispered.

"I left my moose gun out in the car, but I still have my hand gun." I said.

"Great, let's hope we don't need either one of them," he said and cautiously looked out the window. "I do not see anything," he said and then he got a night vision piece out of his bedroom. "Oh, it's only a deer close to the house. Hey, we may as well get started since we are up."

"Great. I do not feel rested. I did not sleep well last night. My pillow and I kept falling off the sofa. I was better off just staying on the floor."

"Sorry about that, but it was the best I could do." He said and went back into his bedroom to get dressed for the day. I wearily got ready for the day also. I really did not feel like going to DC or Arlington, but if it would help, then, go I must. Rick took some of his things out to his car, and I put a few of my clothes in the back seat along with my moose rifle. I really doubted the usefulness of the gun, but I took it anyways. Bruce told me that it was an unregistered gun so I am not sure what that would mean if I were questioned about it. Being a licensed detective, I did have permits to carry weapons, but the big gun may be questionable. We got started around five in the morning.

"I keep my vehicles gassed up." Rick said.

"That is a good idea. I hope we are not driving into trouble."

"I think we will be alright. The person we are going to see is very trusted. I trust him more than anyone else in the government. I have never caught him in a lie."

"Great, he is our next stop?"

"We'll have to get gas, maybe once or twice, but yes, he is our destination in DC."

We stopped several times on the Pennsylvania Turnpike to gas up and to grab something to eat. We pulled into the DC area around three in the afternoon.

"I have to meet him at the Mall. He will be dressed in casual wear, like a tourist with a camera. Straw hat and sneakers, you know the whole deal. I will recognize him from the crowd by his blue flowered shirt. He will accidently drop an envelope on the sidewalk and walk away. I will go and pick it up. It will be just that easy." Rick said with a smile. "After we get the CIA info, we will head to Arlington. It is not very far away, so that will not take long either. After that, we will head home."

"Sounds like a plan. I hope it goes as smoothly as you describe."

"Well, I think we will be alright." Rick replied.

We went into the city and found the Mall. Finding a place to park was another story. We ended up parking in a four-story parking lot that was used by government workers.

"You can come along, but you will need to stay clear of the transaction. I will let you know where to stand."

We went into the Mall and walked a little ways.

"This is good, wait here. I think I see him from here. Just watch," Rick said and walked away. I did as he said and watched him walk toward a tourist. The tourist walked around taking pictures with his camera and dropped something on the ground as he did so. He walked away, aiming his camera at various buildings. Shortly, Rick walked over, picked up the envelope, and looked around as if looking for the owner of the envelope. He shrugged his shoulders and walked back to me.

"Let's go. We need to get out of here in a hurry. I do not think this was a clean drop. There is something wrong." We took off almost in a run back to the car. I was almost exhausted by the time we got into the car. Rick pulled out of the parking space and proceeded to the checkout desk. A car pulled up closely behind him. He paid the parking fee and we left going down N Capitol Street, then to Massachusetts Avenue NW and Pennsylvania Av NW, finally to 22 St NW. I kept a watch for cars following, but I did not see anything suspicious.

"Why did you think it wasn't a clean drop?"

"No reason, just a feeling. So far, my hunch has been wrong. Let's hope it stays wrong."

We proceeded to a rather slummy looking area on the outskirts of Arlington to a small, wood framed, white house. He stopped the car in front of the house and parked there by the curb. He kept the motor running.

"I'll be right back. He knows I'm coming." I watched him go to the front door and walk in without knocking. In about five minutes, he came back out the door with a grin on his face.

He got in the car and said, "That guy is quite a character. He could have been a comedian or someone famous like that, but he chose the cloak and dagger lifestyle. I think he would have been better off in the entertainment business. Here's your stuff."

He handed me a small envelope, and we left. I looked inside the envelope as he found his way back to the Pennsylvania Turn Pike. There was a birth certificate from Ohio, and driver's license with my picture on it. My new name was Clyde Ryner. Also from Ohio, a social security card, a high school diploma from Akron High, a B.S. degree from Ohio State University in teaching. A list of references with phone numbers and address was included. There also was a stamped letter addressed to me giving me a home address on West Market Street, Akron, Ohio, a check stub from an Akron high school for teaching, a car title, and a bank account statement from Bank of America. Most surprisingly, there was five thousand dollars in hundred dollar bills! My money belt was full!

I sat in the passenger seat looking though all of these things in amazement. I put a hundred dollars in my wallet, and carefully put the rest in my money belt. The money belt looked like a regular belt, but it had a secret compartment on the inner side of it that closed with a zipper.

"Wow, this guy is good! How could he do this? Money too!"

"Trust me, he's the best. You will not have any trouble with those credentials and references either. You can get a job now and life, a good and safe life."

"Wow, what about my investigation?"

"You probably should just forget it and move on."

"Yes, but I never lost a case or never failed to bring one to a successful close," I said in reply.

"You are probably dead by now. Your beheaded body that does not have hands or feet, but wearing your clothes with your ID in its pockets probably has been discovered by now. Here, let me turn the news on and see if they say anything about it."

"Whoa! Where did they get the dead body?"

"Not to worry, it's probably some dead Russian."

"Oh, that makes it better?"

"Whatever, it makes it more convincing. No one will be in pursuit of you any longer. Who is going to chase a dead man?"

"I had no idea you could arrange such things?" I said.

"It's who you know. I have many good connections, most of them on the rather dark and shady side, but all of them top secret. I've done things for them, so they do things for me, no questions asked."

"Amazing. It's almost like you were part of the Illuminati or something."

"Hmmn, something like that." He looked in his rear view mirror and shook his head. "There's someone behind us."

I looked back and there was a black Lincoln up close to the back of the car.

"We are in a 1969 Charger 500, my boy. I have one of the great ones with the special 426 high compression Hemi engine and the A833 4-speed manual transmission. An uncommon breed, and very pricy. I do not take to being pushed around! That is why I bought this car. It has saved my life once or twice already. Hang on to your hat. The Lincoln is history!"

"I don't have a hat..."

Suddenly, I heard a deep growl from under the hood and I was thrown back against the seat as this thing took off. I looked back and there was smoke coming from the rear tires, and the Lincoln fell out of sight. I never thought of this car as being a real performance car because Rick had driven it so gently and calmly. Now, I knew that he just liked to baby his special toy.

"You better slow up, Rick, the state patrol is pretty bad on this road." I looked over at the speedometer and it was reading one hundred and forty-five miles an hour! Rick slowly applied the brakes and got it back down to seventy miles an hour. The rest of the trip back to his cabin was without incident.

When we pulled up to the cabin I noticed that there was a car sitting in the driveway. I did not see my car anywhere.

"Oh, there's your new car. Like it?" Rick said.

"It's not exactly a luxury vehicle like what you have." I was looking at a 1967 Chevy Nova with a six cylinder, automatic, green in color. I hate green cars! Rick parked his Charger behind the cabin in the bushes.

I went ahead and put a few of my things in the Nova. We went in and relaxed at the kitchen table. Rick got us some sandwiches from the kitchen and some iced tea. He then opened the envelope and took out the contents. He carefully looked over the top-secret files, and then, one by one, handed them to me. Some were from the Defense Department, some from the Justice Department, others from the office of the CIA. Some pages were redacted, but most were left untouched.

"I think, this explains it all," I concluded after reading the last page. "Or at least part of it."

"All of this is secretive and dangerous information, Zeb. You know these people kill to keep this information from coming out. I would let it go. There is nothing to accomplish now. You are released from the case. Remember you are dead."

"Rick, I appreciate you and what you have done, but I'm not finished yet. See, I can still work and not be detected, so it's even better now."

"You are just stubborn. You can get a job teaching. Don't you understand that? Walk away. If you don't all that I've done for you will be flushed down the toilet, along with your dead body!"

"I will take that in advisement. Trust me, I will be extra cautious now, and be disguised where ever I go."

"Shave your head and grow a beard. That ought to do it."

"That's good advice, maybe tomorrow. Let me think about it."

"You have the couch," Rick said and he went back into his bedroom. I stuffed the CIA file in one of the cushions of the sofa. I was not looking forward to another night on the sofa and that large pillow. I decided to just sleep on the floor. I had a difficult time falling asleep. I wondered how it would be if I chose to live my life as a Clyde Ryner. I guess I could try that, but I really did not want to if I could avoid it. Then, I thought of what I could do with the information from the secret CIA files. That was powerful and disturbing stuff! I drifted off to sleep.

14.

The UFO Connection

A bright white light appeared through the cabin's front window. Startled, I got up and looked outside. The light coming from above brightly lighted just the front yard. Rick rushed out form his bedroom and looked out. We both stood there in silence, not knowing what to say.

"This looks like the same light that I saw at my dad's farmhouse back in Pennsylvania. It was bright and came from the sky, just like this," I said to Rick in a whisper.

"You said it came from some sort of hovering craft?" He asked.

"Yes, but I don't know what it was. It was not like a regular helicopter. It's silent and quick."

"I don't see anyone out there, so I'm going out to take a look." He said. He ran back to his bedroom and brought out some sort of gun.

"Wait, don't you need some sort of protection?" I yelled as he ran out the front door.

"I have this..." he quickly ran off the small front porch and stood just a few feet beyond the last step. I could see him looking up and shading his eyes with his hands in order to get a better look at the flying craft. "I've seen a lot, but I've not seen anything like this. It is not good. If it is one of ours, I did not know we had anything this good. We will find out if it's ours or not." He then raised his gun up to fire. In reply, loud powerful blasts of sound waves came crashing down on him. The impact knocked him to the ground. Lying flat on his back, he raised his gun and began with a burst of bullets. I grabbed my moose gun that my cousin had given me, and joined him. The sound impulses knocked me to the ground also. The roof of the cabin crumbled. I raised my gun and fired a round into the light. Suddenly the light went out, and the sound waves stopped. The mystery craft remained hovering just over the treetops, above the cabin.

"Now, what?" Rick said and looked over at me.

"No clue, but maybe we need to get up and run."

We both got back up on our feet but then we were held by a strong updraft of air. It quickly became so strong that a vacuum began to form around us. I could barely breathe.

"I think we are going up!" Rick said as our feet left the ground.

"This thing has tremendous lifting power! Could it lift bridge parts?" I yelled.

Unexpectedly, everything went dark. I felt that I was flat on my back and that I was in motion.

"Rick! Rick! Where are you?" I shouted. There was no response. Suddenly, I had a pain in my upper arm and I lost consciousness. I am not sure how long I was out, but when I woke up, I found myself securely strapped to a thinly padded table. There was a strange looking light above me. I looked around and it looked like I was in some sort of operating room at a hospital. This was not a hospital, because I had the faint sensation that I was in motion. I lay there quite some time, unable to move. "Hello! Anyone! Where are you? Hello!" I yelled. There was no response from anywhere.

"Rick! Are you there? Somebody get me off this stinking table! This isn't funny!"

I continued to just lie on the table for an indefinite period of time. I got hungry and thirsty. I got more uncomfortable the longer I was strapped onto that table. I caught movement out of the corner of my eye. On the other side of a waist high divide, I saw what looked like an Area 51 creature. It was short, grey, with large cat like eyes and an enlarged cranium. It looked to be wearing a loose robe. Before now, I had totally disregarded such stories, but this looked to be real.

Without turning around, the creature backed up and out of sight. It seemed to glide. I thought that to be strange. The light above me looked like it could be one that was manufactured here on earth. It looked to have a light bulb in it, though different, still a light bulb. The table that I was strapped on, felt like it was covered with plastic, again an earth product. Now, I was suspicious of this set up being fake. However, if it was, why?

Next, I had to figure out how to get out of the straps and off the table. Suddenly, a round port opened above me that revealed the earth at a distance. It was a scary sight!

"Earth man, earth man. Attention please!" a mechanical sounding voice could be heard coming from somewhere.

"You have my attention." I said, remembering some of those cheap flying saucers movies that I had seen from the 1950's. Those were the worst. I suspected that they wanted me to think I was dealing with real space creatures. Since I did not believe in any of that junk, I saw no problem with going along with it to see how things rolled out.

"You are now a prisoner of the tenth planet. We are preparing to take you there, unless you tell us some important things we want to know. If you cooperate, we will put you safely back on the ground..."

"What is it that you want to know?" I asked.

"Where is a man named Zeb Dasher?"

Now, I knew I was not dealing with real space aliens. Apparently, they did not know who I really was.

"Zeb who? I don't know who you are talking about."

"Our findings show that you may be familiar with him by way of his friend named Rick."

"Rick? Rick, Rick, right now I cannot recall anyone by that name. Why do you want to know where this Zeb Dasher is?"

"He has obtained secret information from his government that we are cooperating with. We are assisting them in their effort to find him and recover the stolen documents."

"Well, I have to admit, your methods are far out! I may be able to help you if you undo these awful straps. I need food and water. If I get that, I will cooperate with you." There was no reply.

In a few minutes, the straps clicked open, and I was loose. A door opened on the other side of the room. I could see that it was a bathroom, so I went in. There I found clothing lay neatly out on the sink. I used the bathroom, took a shower and put on the fresh clothing that was provided. The clothing was loose fitting as if the size was uncertain. I felt a little better. The door opened back into the original room with the table on which I was strapped. I walked back in. There was a plate of food on the table, freshly cooked. There was mac and cheese, a hamburger, a handful of potato chips, and a tall glass of iced tea.

"So, my alien friends, who does the cooking for you? How do you shop? What grocery store do space aliens use? I'm just wondering." I sat on the tabletop and ate my provisions.

After I finished eating, I said, "You can all stop with the space alien thing now. I'm not buying it."

The mechanical voice came back from a speaker located in the ceiling. "We have given you what you asked; now we need your cooperation. Where is Zeb Dasher, please?"

I looked around for possible ways out. "Let me think for a minute." I said stalling for time. I decided to see where that alien dummy went that I saw on the other side of the room divide. I got off the table and looked behind the room divide. There was nothing to be seen on that side. I walked around the divide and pushed on the wall and it opened to narrow passageways that lead to a regular looking door.

I opened it and I found myself in a very large warehouse. The building that I had just come out of had another door. I looked back to see the large metallic saucer that I had just came out of. I opened it and I saw a man sitting behind a desk with a large bank of computers beside it.

"Wheeling? Got it. We can coordinate some pieces to the shipyard in Norfolk. I will get the same transport that we used the last time. Thank you, sir." The officer said and hung up the phone.

I stepped in and tapped him on the shoulder. He turned around and was startled to see me.

"Now, Mr. Alien, you are going to tell me who you are and who you work for."

"Whoa! I don't know what you mean."

"You have two seconds to give me an honest answer before I take you and this place apart."

"Okay, no need to get violent. I am Commander John Smathers. I work for U.S. Navy."

"U.S. Navy? What in the world are you doing looking into Zed Dasher things?"

"We are intelligence gathering. All I can tell you is that we would like to speak with Mr. Dasher."

"So, what's the deal with the flying saucer gig?"

"I am not authorized to give out that information, Mr. Ryner. That is all I can tell you."

"It's some sort of lift machine isn't it? A secret spy device that looks like a flying saucer is my guess."

Through some sort of glitch in communications, this man and his part of the operation thought I was Clyde Ryner.

"I need my ID and wallet back."

"Sorry, I can't give that to you."

Just then, I gave him a right cross punch to the jaw and he fell out of his chair and fell limply to the floor.

"Sorry, about that, but there was no other way." I looked around the room and found my phony ID and paperwork stashed on top on a filing cabinet. I stuffed that in my pockets and left. The warehouse looked to be nearly empty, except for the three military vehicles parked near one of the garage doors. There was a small office on the opposite side of the building that was lit up indicating that there were people in it. I walked over to the three vehicles. There were keys in the ignition in all of them. I took the keys out of two of them and got into the third one. It started right up. I threw it into gear and drove out.

15.

Escape

I had no idea of where I was and therefore did not have any idea of where to go. My guess was that there was something in Wheeling, West Virginia that I needed to see. I just knew that I needed to get out of that warehouse and on the road. I would have to ditch the truck soon since the police would be looking for it. This warehouse was located out in farm country. The land was rolling hills. I kept on driving until I saw a sign. Cumberland straight ahead, ten miles. Now, I knew I was in Maryland. Pennsylvania was just to the north. I decided to head to West Virginia. I just wanted out of both Pennsylvania and Maryland. I stopped in Cumberland at a truck stop. There I parked the military vehicle and walked into the store.

I sat down at the serving bar and ordered a burger, fries and a soft drink. The trucker next to me was having a plate of spaghetti.

"Where are you headed?" I asked in between bites.

"Wheeling, West Virginia. I have a couple of cars to drop off before I head back to Lordstown, Ohio."

"I have a friend who lives in Youngstown, which isn't far from Lordstown."

"I know where it's at."

"What's your name?" I asked.

"Mark Johnson and you?"

"Clyde Ryner."

"Do you think that you could give me a ride to Wheeling?"

"I can since I'm an independent operator. If the freight company employed me, I would not have that freedom. No rider is their policy. I'm my own boss, so yes, I can give you a ride."

"Well, that is great. I appreciate the ride." We both sat there and finished our meals. He got up and went back to the restroom. I turned in my seat and looked out the front window. There were several military vehicles pulled up next to the one that I had driven. There were men searching through it for something. Mark Johnson came out of the restroom.

"You ready?" he said.

"Sure am," I said.

We both went to the cashier and paid our tabs.We walked out to his tractor-trailer. It was a nice new International Harvester, thirteen speed, with dual exhaust. We both jumped in and he started it up. I looked back as we were pulling out and saw that several of the military personnel were walking to the shop that we had just left. This was a car carrier, and Mark had three new cars on the trailer destined for Wheeling. After that, he was headed back to Lordstown for another load. I was glad that I was able to get this ride, because it surely saved the day for me.

I sat back and relaxed. He played the radio and talked on his CB at the same time. I knew West Virginia was mountainous but the highway that we were on smoothed out some of the worst of them. After a while I drifted off to sleep, but was awakened by Mark downshifting the truck.

"What's up?" I asked.

"Onion, on the CB just told me that the state troopers have a road block just ahead. They are pulling tractor-trailers over and searching them for something. I am getting off here at this exit to avoid delays. Those people can hold a tractor-trailer up for hours. I'm going around them if I can."

I was now uncertain about what lay ahead.

"Those boys may have the side roads closed off also. I'm about to find out," he said as we turned off the highway on to a country road. "Don't worry, I know my way around. We will be there before you know it."

We proceeded uninhibited to Wheeling. He was right; he certainly knew his way around. I got off at the car dealership and bid him good-bye. He was a good man, and he probably would have taken me back to Youngstown if I had stuck with him. I did not think that it was a good idea to go back to Rick's cabin outside of Youngstown. They were probably waiting for me there. I still had my CIA files and my entire phony ID, so I was determined to follow through with my investigation and see it to the end. I hope that that did not mean my end also.

I had money, some in my money belt, and some in my wallet, so I rented a car there using my bogus ID. I was concerned that my new ID was no longer a cover for me, but that is all that I had. According to what Rick had told me, the person Zeb Dasher had been erased. It was rather difficult to get used to the name Clyde Ryner, but that was an adjustment that I would have to make. I decided to look around the city. I drove around looking at one section of the city at a time. I worked my way from the center of the city to the outskirts. I was not sure of what I was looking for, and I could just be wasting my time.

I came to a very large scrap yard, and I decided to drive in to look around. I pulled the car over at the check-in house. I got out and then I saw it. There were large sections of steel still assembled behind the building. It looked like part of a large bridge. I walked behind the building and got a closer look. Yes, this was it! I had walked across the Clarion River Bridge several times, and this definitely looked like it could be part of it. If that were true, how did it get here, and why is it here? Then, further, where is the rest of it? I went inside the check-in house and approached the man behind the counter.

"Hello, how may I help you?" the man asked

"Yes sir, can you tell me where that bridge section came from?"

"Oh, no sir, we don't have records of that. I think it has off an old collapsed bridge, maybe from somewhere around here. Why? Do you want to purchase some of the steel off it? I can give you a good price."

I played along, "How much per ton?"

"It depends on how many tons you want to buy. We will give a substantial discount for large purchases."

"Can you tell me how long it has been sitting back there?"

"It doesn't make any difference. The steel is in excellent condition.

"I see. Therefore, you do not know where it came from or how long it has been here. How do you know it hasn't been exposed to sea salt, or salt air?"

"Oh, you can just look at it and tell that. This thing must have spanned over a fresh water river. There is no evidence of salt corrosion anywhere. We are too far in land to get any of that. You should know that."

"Fresh water river? Any idea just from how far away things are brought here?"

"No, we don't ask those kinds of questions, but from the size of the beams, it would have cost a fortune to ship all that steel. So, my guess, it didn't come from very far away."

"So, why didn't it go to a steel mill to be melted down instead of here?"

"Don't know that either buddy. Say, you ask many questions. Are you interested in purchasing any of it or not? I have other things to do."

"Okay, I think we can do business. May I have your business card?" I asked.

The man went over to a desk and pulled a card out of the desk drawer. He brought it over and handed it to me.

"There you go. Just give me a call. John told me few minutes ago – John is our boss – that we have received a call about that steel from a government contractor. So, if you are going to do anything with it, you better not drag your feet. That contractor may get it first. They pay good money."

I took his card and left. Yes, I have been looking for this place. Now, I had the actual bridge, at least part of it. Then, again, I may have a problem proving that this section was part of the Clarion Bridge. Against my better judgment, I left and drove back to Youngstown. I wanted the things that I had left behind at Rick's cabin. I parked the car halfway down Rick's driveway and walked the rest of the way. I was not sure what or whom I would find there. I hid in the thick bushes until I was sure that there was no one around. I cautiously walked into the cabin.

The roof and been collapsed but the ceiling was still intact. I went all through the small cabin and concluded that no one was there. I was surprised that the Feds had abandoned the site already, if indeed they had. I just needed some of the things out of what little I had left in the cabin. I got the CIA folder out of the sofa and put it in the green Nova. I went around back to the Charger well hidden in the bushes. I peeked in the front window.

"Surprise meeting you here!" Rick said as he sat up in the car seat.

"Where have you been?"

"We were both taken out of here by a government surveillance craft. You don't remember?"

"Remember what? I do have a vague recall of a spacecraft or something. I don't remember anything after that."

"I think you have been drugged, Rick."

"I wouldn't doubt it. I am surprised that they brought me back here. I should be in some forgotten prison in Saudi Arabia. This goes against standard protocol, but no matter. I am glad I did not end up like that. Maybe it was my past duty with the agency that spared me, I don't know."

"I found the bridge."

"Bridge? Really, where?"

"Wheeling, West Virginia. I need to have a way of confirming that it is the same bridge. I think it may have manufacture numbers on the steel beams, but I'm not sure."

"Hold on, Zeb. One way to be sure is to check to see if it is radioactive. If that spike that you found at the bottom of the river was radioactive, the bridge probably is also."

"You are right, Rick."

"Right as rain. I have a small government issued Giger counter in the trunk of this car. I have all sorts of junk back there. Anyways, we need to test that bridge."

"Okay, that would be as soon as possible then. They are talking about a government contractor taking what's left of it any day now." I replied. "How about now? Let's go now."

"I don't know, Zeb. My head is still sort of swimming from those drugs. I sure was imagining things. Little grey men and spaceships, wow, that is just off the chain."

"Well, I can drive. Let's get in my green Nova and go."

"Not in your life. We are taking the Charger or we are not going. That Nova cannot outrun a chicken, okay. You will just have to drive my car until I feel up to it. Now, go get your stuff," Rick insisted. I hurried and transferred my things to the back seat of his Charger. I got in the front driver's seat and he leaned back in the front passenger seat. 'Just baby it until you get used to it. You will be okay. I see you have a rental car, I'll turn that in for you if need be."

"Thanks.. I used to have a Chevelle with a 396 in it. That thing would fly. I'm sure I can handle this thing." I started it up and we pulled out of the driveway. Back to Wheeling it was!

16.

Findings at Edgewood.

We rolled down the highway without any incident. I kept my eyes open for state troopers, but I saw none. There was a lot of difference in the land between Youngstown and Wheeling. Once a person came into that area, the hills kept getting steeper. It was pretty country in the fall. The hills became decorated with autumn beauty at that time. It was worth the drive just to view the scenery.

We came into Wheeling and drove right to the scrapyard. The bridge portion was still there.

"You were right, there it is!" Rick said as he woke up from his nap. "Let me get the Giger Counter out of the back," he said and then went to the trunk of the car and lifted the lid. He took some time going through all the things back there. It certainly was packed, then, he found it. The Giger Counter was not much more than a little grey-blue box with an attached sensor. As soon as he turned it on it started clicking.

"Whoa, there you go. It's already clicking!" he said as he walked toward the bridge. "It is getting louder the closer I come to it! It is definitely highly radioactive!"

"Wow, stay back away from it. It could be dangerous to your health." I said.

"That is amazing. Whatever it met must have been some strong stuff. This counter is almost pegged standing way back here."

"I need to warn the workers inside the building that it may be a health hazard." I said.

"Right, something this strong could easily poison someone."

I went inside and told the man behind the counter. He listened to me and acted not interested. He just acknowledged what I said and then went and sat back down at his desk. He would let the boss know, is all he said. I left and joined Rick outside.

"Okay, they know, but they don't seem too concerned about it." I said to Rick.

"Well, that is their decision. We still need to positively identify this as part of the bridge, however. There must be some sort of number or ID somewhere on the bridge that could do that," Rick replied.

"Well, I don't think that is necessary. I mean, how many radioactive bridges are there running around? Just this one I would dare say."

Rick went back to the trunk of the car and pulled out a pair of binoculars from the trunk.

"Humor me, okay. Let me just scan over it with this." He leaned against the front fender of the Charger and slowly looked over each of the parts of the bridge. "Ah, there we go, look at this!" he said and handed me the binoculars. "There on the lower beam it says something that may interest you."

It was part of a bent sign that the highway department had put on the bridge at one time. It said, "The Clarion River Bridge has been inspected by..." The sign had been torn in half but what was still there told all that we needed.

"Oh boy, would you look at that?" I said with joy in my heart. "It doesn't get much better than that. However, that is not the complete story. Like why is it here? What happened to it? What's the deal with the radioactivity?"

"We need to take a closer look at all those files you have. I'm sure there's information in there that we can use." Rick took several pictures of the sign on the bridge. "That helps."

"Well, Rick, I did read over the files, well most of them. There are a lot of lines that have been blackened out and not readable." We got back into the car. I pulled the files off the back seat and looked through them.

"Here let me look at them. Those things are loaded with government double talk. Let me see if I can translate some of it for you."

He sat in the seat and poured over each page for a while. "Okay, I have a light that will show what is on the other side of the redactions. In order to get some needed facts, I'll have to use it." He reached into the glove box and pulled out a bottle containing a liquid that he brushed over the redacted sections. Then, he got a light out of the trunk that looked like a flashlight but it emitted a strange blue light on the paper. He carefully went over each line and wrote above the redaction what was under it.

"Now, all this is a lot clearer. Some of it even makes a little sense," he said with a smile and handed the file back to me.

"So, the bridge was raised in the middle of the night by the government? But why all the secrecy?"

"Good question. They are hiding something very important and probably without any doubt, very top secret. Whatever Project X-Caliber X is, it is now located at the Edgewood Arsenal in Maryland, but originated at the Aberdeen Proving Grounds not too far from there." Rick said.

"So, what would anything from there be doing going across the Clarion Bridge?"

"Since, its top secret, we will probably never know." Rick said and shrugged his shoulders. "The info here seems rather vague as to what the project really is. It must be some sort of secret weapon.

"What would it take to get on the Edgewood Arsenal grounds?"

"Oh, we could get on as visitors, but we would be very limited in where we could go and to whom we may talk with." Rick said.

"Well, we are getting nowhere just sitting here. Next stop, Edgewood." I said.

"I don't think we will gain much by going all the way down there," Rick protested.

"We are making progress. We need just a little more information before we can bring this thing to a close."

"Great, I'm driving." Rick replied. He drove to the Pennsylvania Turnpike and we made good time. With him driving, we were there in six hours. Riding down Highway One and then into Bel-Air, Maryland was a nice peaceful, scenic ride. I enjoyed seeing Pennsylvania Dutch country. Edgewood was just a short hop from there.

We stopped at the gate and got our visitor's pass. We pulled up to the welcome center. We were not permitted to go out into the various buildings, but the canteen and gift shop were open to us. We went into the on-base restaurant and sat at a table. Both of us ordered cold-cut sandwiches and an order of potato chips. As we sat there, several officers came in and sat next to us. We could hear some of their conversation even though they spoke quietly...

"From the inspection report, the outside housing is ruptured and not repairable," one of the officers said in a low, just above whispering voice.

"We will need to get a crew on dismantling it from the rocket engine, then, and shipping the upper section with the radioactive material back to Texas. A C5 A transport needs to be used, not a tractor-trailer, for crying out loud. Col. Alberts was badly mistaken to authorize that form of transportation for such a high level project," whispered the other man.

"Too bad this thing is ruined. It is part of our only advanced rotator nuclear delivery weapon. There is nothing else like it in the world. It simply spun and threw out cobalt warheads by the hundreds as it passed over a target nation. It is a work of genius. " The other officer quietly replied in dismay. "Just one of those could destroy an entire country, not just a city."

"The nice thing was, really, that each dirty cobalt warhead could be independently targeted. It could throw a warhead out that had a range of a thousand miles in any direction. Do you think the project will be cancelled now? I don't think it will."

"That is up to the select House Appropriations Sub-Committee, the Pentagon and of course the CIA, but any set back throws a dim light on a secret project."

"Well, it's too late to worry about any of that. The expense of the one ruined X Caliber X will certainly be negatively viewed. Too bad."

We finished our cold cut sandwiches and quietly left the restaurant.

"Well, that was a real stroke of luck, Zeb! Now, we know more about the project, and why. What else do you need? It seems like my contacts in the CIA should have been able to tell me about this."

"I don't know, but maybe that will wrap things up as far as I'm concerned." I said and we both got into the car. Rick started it up and we proceeded to the main gate to leave.

We were stopped by the soldiers at the gate and then forced to park the car and get out. There was a black box van that came shortly and picked us up. We were separated and taken to separate prison cells by armed guards.

17.

Gone for a Swim

I was kept in a single locked cell for several days with no visitors. I received food and water through a small door built into the steel door of entry. No one talked to me, not even the guards. They ignored me. I wondered how Rick was doing. I wondered how they could do this to a civilian. Just locking me in prison with no questions, no trial or sentence pronounced on any charge, no defense attorney was offered, nothing. It was very unconstitutional. Apparently, these people operated above the law, or the Constitution meant nothing to them.

The fourth day, two guards came and escorted me out of the building, and transported me to an airfield. There, I was put on a military transport plane. I was handed a parachute and told to put it on. I was not sure that I liked the idea, but I have skydived before, so I was not afraid of it. We took off and flew east, out over the ocean for about an hour. There were very few people onboard the plane, just the pilot, copilot, and two soldiers. I wondered what happened to Rick, but more importantly, what was going to happen to me.

The two soldiers took me by my arms and pulled me to the side door of the plane. One opened the door. The ocean was far below.

"Okay, smart guy, jump," one of them demanded. The other soldier pushed me in the direction of the open door.

"Over the ocean? You must be out of your minds!" I yelled.

"You are going to disappear, one way or another, now jump."

"So, why give me a parachute?"

"The parachute is for your own protection. You would be killed on impact without it. You need a more fitting death, like one of playing with the sharks for a while. I understand that they are friendly in this area."

They both grabbed me and shoved me out the door. The parachute opened and I landed in the cool water of the Atlantic Ocean. I watched as the plane made a wide turn and went back to where it came from. I am a good swimmer, so I folded my parachute up into as small of a ball as I could and stuck it in the bag that it came out of the best I could. The parachute really did not fit very well with the water added to it, but I decided to drag it along for as far as I could think it may help with the sharks. I found out shortly that it was not really a good idea, and more of a hindrance than I could bear. I kept it on but it felt like it was going to be my downfall. I swam and rested, I treaded water on my back, then I swam some more. I kept on moving. I was afraid that if I stopped, sharks would gather around me. I would not be able to either get rid of the sharks or defend myself from them if they did come, so I kept on moving. The parachute may act as a blind if they did come, but I was not confident that the blind would be very effective.

I marked the days that I swam, and each day that went by, I got slower and more exhausted. I did not see any sharks come around me, which was amazing. I figured that would not last. When I rested, I took the parachute out and let it spread out over a large area, with me in the middle. It seemed to keep the fish away pretty well. As long as there was no blood in the water, I was not in any immediate danger. Once or twice on the fourth evening while resting, did a shark come up to the floating parachute. It could tell that the chute was not a living creature, so it went away after a brief inspection.

On my sixth day of swimming and floating, a shark swam below me for a short distance. It shadowed me for a while, but then it swam away. I was beyond starving by this time, and my tongue was so dry it was stuck to the roof of my mouth. I figured that I may last another day at most, but I did not give up. I feebly kept on. A little progress, then, rest, and then, going again. I refused to give up.

On the seventh day, I was next to being delirious, almost blind, and very exhausted when I saw a large cruise ship coming my way. It was one of those luxury liners that took people to the Virgin Islands and ports south. It was headed straight for me so I waved my arms and tried to yell the best I could. My throat was so dry that all I could do was make a noise. I saw some passengers at the front of the ship look and point at me. I was saved! The ship slowed and stopped just past me. A small boat was lowered over the side and two men rowed out and helped me on board. I was taken to sickbay on the upper deck and given liquids and nourishment. I was kept there for two days, and regained my strength. They gave me some fresh clothing that normally was given to employees. So, I looked like I worked for the cruise line. I was told that it was all that they had at the time. It had to do while my clothes went to the laundry. I even asked for an official hat to keep my hair from being blown by the tropical winds there. It would keep the sun off my sunburned face. They gave me an attractive hat, which I did wear. I was careful to put my money belt on, remembering the money that was stored in there.

We stopped at several Virgin Islands seaports and some of the passengers got off as tourists. I did not get off, and was not interested in looking like a tourist. I still wore the cruise uniform, since my clothes would not be back from the laundry until late in the afternoon. I stood on deck beside a deck steward near the boarding plank as people went ashore. Two men in black suits and ties walked up the plank and asked if there was a passenger on board by the name of Zeb Dasher. They showed the steward a picture of me. Then, amazingly, enough they showed the picture to me. I just shook my head and said, "No, I've never seen this man." The hat and uniform made it look like I was a crewmember and the stubby beard that I wore made them not even seriously look at me. They turned and thanked us and walked back down the plank and went to the next cruise ship docked close to this one.

"Hmmn, I wonder what all of that was about," the steward said.

"No idea," I said and went back to my ships quarters. Now I knew they were checking to see if I had survived somehow. If they caught me, they would finish the job. That meant that I could not get back into the states the usual way. I would have to find a back door in. With my money, I could possibly rent a boat to the mainland. I could not fly in or take a regular passenger ship, because they would be checking those. Perhaps the only other option would be the long way around, through the Mexican/Texas border via the Rio Grande. That would be an extreme measure, but the safest. I left the room and went to the guest information desk.

"Can you tell me if there's a ship that leaves the Virgin Islands and goes to Mexico?" I asked the young woman at the desk.

She opened several books and leafed through them, finally stopping on a page.

"Yes sir, there's one that leaves tomorrow morning for Cancun at 8. Pier number five, sir. Tickets are through Hughes Travel Agency, on Pier Five."

"Cost?"

"Subject to change, sir. You will have to ask them."

"No matter, thank you," I said. "Where is Pier Five?"

"Go down the exit plank and then go left along the bay front. It will be two piers down from here. You will see their building."

I left and went to Pier Five. The Hughes Travel Agency was not busy and they were glad to sell me a one-way ticket to the seaport at Cancun for several hundred dollars. From there, I would have to rent a car to drive to the states. Considering that what I had left in my money belt this trip may break me financially. I went back to the cruise ship and found that the laundry had delivered my clean clothes back to my room. I showered and got into my regular clothes. I put my wallet and my important paper work in my pockets. Afterwards, I went to the ships recreation room and played a few games, and then retired to the large dining room area. I got a full meal there since I was not sure about the quality of food I would find on the road through Mexico. After that, I went back to my room and settled in for the night. Tomorrow may prove to be a long day. I was uncertain about how safe I would be traveling through Mexico. I would worry about that later. Now, I needed to relax and sleep.

18.

Down Mexico Way

The boat ride to Cancun was rather rocky, since there was a tropical storm in the area. It took four days to get from the Virgin Islands to the port at Cancun since the boat stopped at a small island. The food on the ship was not very good, so I was glad to get off when we got to Mexico At the port, there were taxi's there waiting to take passengers into Cancun. They would take anyone to the hotel that sponsored them. The name of the sponsoring hotel was printed on the side of the Taxi, so you got into the taxi that went to the hotel that you wanted to stay. I picked the Hilton, and was whisked to a towering hotel fairly close to the beach. They had nice facilities, including an indoor swimming pool. I got a room on the sixth floor. It was a small suite, so I had a kitchen, and two rooms with one full sized bathroom. The welcome AC worked really well, so I enjoyed that.

I planned to stay only one day. The hotel exchanged a one hundred dollar bill for pesos. It looked like a lot of money. I found out from the hotel desk clerk that I could rent a car from Avis that had an office on the first floor in the hotel. I went there, next and rented a car with unlimited mileage with auto insurance. It was a rather pricy arrangement no matter what vehicle I chose. Their first offer was a clean 1972 Caprice, fully loaded. A luxury car would give me a good ride. I anticipated the roads further in Mexico to be not paved or very smooth. Instead of the Caprice, I chose the six cylinder Jeep that had AC. Jeeps are not known for delivering a very smooth, comfortable ride, but the roads were not going to be comfortable anyway. The four-wheel drive may come in handy, so that was my choice. I filled out the insurance papers, and the assistant drove the Jeep up to the front door of the hotel. I parked the Jeep on the side parking lot of the hotel, and went back to my room. Tomorrow would be the start of a long journey. My immediate destination was going to be Texas. I had gotten a road map from Avis, so I spent the evening looking at the map and figuring the best way to get out of Mexico. Some of the roads were marked as under construction, some unfinished, some were complete dead-ends. It looked like it would be best to go to Merida next, and follow the coastal roads if I could. I may have to make my own road part of the way. My Spanish would definitely be tested during the trip.

In the morning, I left the hotel and started my journey to Texas. The road to Merida was roughly paved, and had unmarked speed bumps on the road, which were quite jarring. I found that the best speed on those roads was between thirty-five and forty-five miles an hour. Merida had some nice historic sites, and was a feast for any photographer. It took me about five and a half hours to go from Cancun to Merida. I stopped there to get some fine Mexican food at a nice restaurant. I still had a half of a day to go before the sun went down, so I left there and continued on my journey. I arrived in Campeche a little after five. I found a fairly nice room in a moderate looking hotel there. The rate was very reasonable. Renting a room is cheaper off the tourist trail. I found out a little later that the road going west was still unfinished. The map showed it to be under construction. Tomorrow, I would have to drive south to hit a road that was supposedly complete that went west to Villahermosa.

In the morning, I checked out of the hotel and found a Gulf gasoline station a few blocks away. I filled the Jeep up, and bought a spare ten-gallon gas can that I also filled up. I placed that in the back, and proceeded south. The road was narrow, bumpy and dusty. It was dirt only part of the way. The weather was hot and dry. I was glad it was not the rainy season. That would have been a real mess on the dirt roads. It was almost lunchtime when I approached a paved intersection. According to the map, this is where I turned to the right to go west. There was a car sitting in the middle of the intersection with its hood raised. I slowed down and went around it. A woman got out of the car and tried to wave me down to stop. I had read that it was a common technique of highway robbers to pose as breakdown victims. I felt badly for her if she was truly broken down, but I best not take chances. I may not live through a hold up. Some of these thieves were cutthroats. I had no weapons to defend myself. I did know how to defend myself, but I would not stand a chance if the thieves were armed. I kept going and it got dark as I drove. The road seemed to get worse. I had to slow up because there were great ridges in the dirt that were extremely rough. I came to a dried up creek bed that had no bridge. I was glad that I was in a four-wheel drive Jeep when I got to the other side.

I drove until almost midnight. I pulled well off to the side of the road to rest. There was absolutely no traffic on this road. As a matter of fact, the only car that I had seen was the broken down car back at the intersection. That was miles ago. I could tell that horses had been on this road, probably more so than gasoline-powered vehicles. As a precaution, I pulled the Jeep further off the road, and down a small hill. It would not be easily seen if someone did come along during the night. I took my gas can out of the back and emptied it into the Jeep's tank. I did that so that I would not have to worry about running out of gas when I needed to leave. I could probably go another two hundred miles without stopping now. I thought that I must be getting fairly close to Villahermosa, but I did not see any city lights lighting up the sky to the west. I took a blanket and pillow out of the back of the Jeep that I had purchased from a shop at the Hilton and climbed under the Jeep. All my valuables went with me under the vehicle. I would be protected from rain that way. Anyone coming by would not immediately see me under the Jeep in the darkness. That proved to be a good idea because around three in the morning someone came up to the Jeep on horseback and went all through the Jeep looking for valuables. They found nothing. The would-be thief even tried to raise the hood of the Jeep to get the battery out, but it had come with locks on it. After a while, he got back on his horse and road off. I figured that he may be back later with a tow truck to take the whole vehicle, but I would be gone before then. Shortly after the raider left I put my things back in the Jeep and started on my journey west. It would be daybreak soon, and I should be in the next town before then.

As I entered Villahermosa, I saw a tow truck go past me going the other way. I knew where they were going, and was glad that they would be disappointed. My charity does not run that deep. I found a nice place to eat for breakfast. They had very reasonable prices and polite service. The menu actually had an English page, so I ordered from it. Afterwards I went outside and looked around. I was the only American to be seen. Some people walked by looking at me as if I were some celebrity or something. Refreshed, I got back in my Jeep and again headed out on the road. My next stop would be Coatzacoalcos. I prided myself in what I imagined to be making good time in my travels. I hoped to be there by around lunchtime. The roads proved to be no better than before, and were mostly dirt. It looked like very few automobiles were ever brought out on the road I was on. There were definite wagon wheel ruts in the road. I had to drive slowly to avoid the large sinkholes. It did not look like the road had ever been repaired or maintained.

Suddenly, in my rear view mirror I saw three men on horseback rapidly approaching me. I pressed the accelerator pedal to the floor. The result was being bounced high out of my seat. I managed to put my seat belt on and resumed at that pace. I did forty-five miles an hour, a pace that a horse could not maintain for any great distance. I shortly out ran them. I could see in the mirrors that they had stopped and turned around. That confirmed my fear that they were really after my vehicle and me. I would have to stop and get gasoline at the next town.

As I came to the top of a small hill, an old pickup truck pulled out on to the road right in front of me. I slammed on the brakes and managed to swerve around him. I accelerated away, figuring that it was another highwayman looking for an easy victim. The pickup up turned and came after me. My Jeep was not very fast, but it was good on rough terrane. I had the pedal to the floor but the truck inched closer as we went along. Suddenly we came to another dried creek bed. I kept the pedal to the floor and flew over most of it. The back wheels caught the far bank and I immediately picked up speed on the other side. I looked back and the pickup did not fair too well. The front end of the truck slammed into the far creek bed and came to an abrupt stop. After that the road became paved, and then widened. I was coming into a large sprawling city.

Coatzacoalcos.was a welcome sight. It had good, paved streets and many hotels being it was on the coast. I did not see any of the old world Mayan monuments that I thought might be there, or much even in old Spanish type housing, this city was surprisingly modern. I filled up my Jeep and spare gas can at a gasoline station. I picked out a nice restaurant to eat my lunch and again the food was good. I always chose to drink the wine at a restaurant and never the water. Only the wine could be trusted to be pure even at a nice restaurant. I still had a half a day of driving in front of me, so I lounged at the restaurant for a little over an hour. After that, I was back out on the road. I decided to skip Veracruz and go straight into Jalapa. It was a bigger city and I would have better places to stay.

I spent the night there in a nice room, ate breakfast, and was back on the road by seven in the morning. I filled my gasoline tank, spare gas can, and I decided to push on through to Ponza Rica. There, I again refreshed myself at a nice restaurant, and filled my tanks back up. I was back on the road again by two in the afternoon. I made it to Tampico by evening and rested there that night. I got an early start at six the next morning and went on to Cuidad Victoria. It was going to be my last stop before hitting Matamoros on the Mexican-American border. I was anxious to finally get to the border. Brownsville was just on the other side of the river.

When I came out of the restaurant that I had stopped at in Cuidad Victoria and walked to my rented Jeep, two Mexican police officers stopped me. They had noticed the Avis Rent-A-Car sticker on the back of the Jeep. I surmised that they wanted some sort of paper work. I showed them my Avis rental agreement, and they both shook their heads. They wanted something else. Then, they again began explaining what they wanted, and finally I figured that they wanted some immigration document, to prove I came to Mexico legally.

"Look, I came into Mexico from the Virgin Islands. I landed in Cancun. They asked for no paperwork there, so I have none," I explained.

"No? None?" one of the police officers said. The other grabbed my arm. "Estás bajo arresto."

"Arresto?

"Si, Pagar la multa"

"What?"

"One hundred American dollars, US." One of them said and held out his hand.

I had five hundred dollars out in my wallet at the time because I was going to exchange some of it for pesos to buy gasoline. I took a hundred dollars out of my wallet and handed it to one of the police officers.

"Each." The other police officer said and held out his hand.

"Each?" I grimly pulled another one hundred dollars out of my wallet and handed it to the other police officer. He snatched it out of my hand and smiled.

"Veto," the other one said and waved his hand. They both turned and walked away. I was relieved to see them leave. It could have been worse. I had heard horror stories of people being robbed by the police and ended up in prison after they had nothing left to pay. Sometimes it required an American relative bailing them out and retrieving them out of the country just to get back into the states. I did not waste any time getting out of town and on the road to Matamoros.

It was late in the afternoon, before sunset, that I arrived at Matamoros. I got a room at a hotel on what was called "The Strip." The Strip was the road on which the bridge to Brownsville was located. I slept in a fairly nice room that night, and in the morning, the clerk directed me to the nearest Avis facility so that I could turn in my Jeep. It was also located on the strip less than a block away. The Avis man told me in English that renting vehicles in Mexico was not popular due to the conditions of the roads, and because the roads were dangerous. I had to agree with that. He told me several stories of how some Americans were robbed and killed in Mexico by inadvertently driving into certain "cartel" areas. Mexican gangs controlled much of the countryside. He was amazed that I came all the way from Cancun safely.

"You are a miracle, my friend. I do not think anyone in their right minds would have tried to drive from Cancun to here. By all odds, your body parts should be bleaching in the sands somewhere between here and there," He smiled and handed me my proof of return of the vehicle. He kept the deposit on the vehicle for what he called maintenance. "Maybe, because it was a Jeep that you were driving, and you had the nerve to drive it straight through some bad lands, they left you alone. They thought you to be one bad hombre. You must be blessed by the saints."

"Well, I'm just glad that I will be walking across the bridge into the states, soon." I said and shook his hand.

"Now, I have something to tell others about, how that a gringo drove all the way here from Cancun, and lived. Sir, thank you, and if you are ever in Mexico again, come back." He said with a big smile. "And bring more money."

I left and walked back to the hotel, gathered up my things and checked out.

19.

A Surprise in Texas

I walked across the bridge into Texas and felt a definite relief once I standing on U.S. soil again. Brownsville was a large modern city. I checked into a nice hotel there, and got a room on the second floor. I had a nice view of the parking lot from my window. I freshened up and made my way to the phone. I called Rick.

"Zeb? That is you isn't it? What in the world are you doing in Texas?" He immediately asked when he picked up the phone.

"What? How did you know it was me, and how do you know that I'm in Texas? That is unreal!"

"You forget, Zeb, I'm in the intelligence business. I know things."

"What happened? When did they let you out of the lock up in Maryland?" I asked.

"I was only briefly detained. After being questioned, I was released. I came back here and have been waiting to hear from you."

"Are you sure your line isn't tapped? Seems like it was at one time."

"No, I ran my own security check on my line, and it's clean. So, what's up with you?"

"I just got back from my vacation to Cancun. It was a nice trip. I'll have to tell you about it some time."

"Cancun is nice. I was there a couple of years ago. I'm glad to hear that you are taking time to relax."

"Right, I'm going to be here a few days, and then I'm going back to Clarion and get this mess straightened out. I want to get my life back."

"Zeb, you are dead, remember? It' best if you leave it that way. You have your new life and freedom, now. Don't throw it away."

"Rick, I am who I am. Phony paperwork doesn't change who I am."

"Hmmn, you could at least try. Your life does depend on it."

"So, why is the government trying to get rid of me?"

"I can't tell you that, but think about it. You are trying to delve into some top secret projects to which you don't have legal access."

"Yes, but to be dumped out into the Atlantic Ocean, I mean, really."

"Atlantic Ocean? What are you talking about?"

"Never mind that. It just was part of my vacation that I'll tell you about sometime." I was beginning to doubt the wisdom of my call to Rick. I perhaps, inadvertently had given my position away to the federal government. "Well, Rick, I'll be seeing you. I'll keep in touch."

"Do you need me to come and pick you up?"

"No, that won't be necessary. I'll let you know, Good-bye, Rick."

I hung up the phone. I was not sure about Rick. Was he acting like a double agent now? He may have made a deal when we were in lock-up, just to get out. So, I tentatively put him on the untrustworthy list. I hated to do that, but sometimes you have to do things that you do not like. I relaxed and took a nap. Afterwards, I went for a walk into the city. I stopped into a men's clothing store and bought some new shirts, pants and one suit. Then, I went next door to a shoe and luggage store and bought a new pair of shoes and a suitcase. I took all of that back to my room at the hotel. I packed the suitcase with my new clothes and my paperwork Next I went down to the desk clerk and found out where the nearest bus station was. Luckily, I could buy bus tickets there at the desk and the Greyhound bus stopped there three times a day. I was thrilled. I bought a one-way ticket to San Antonio and went back to my room.

There I relaxed in front of the television for a while. The bus left the hotel at seven in the morning, so I made the best of my stay. The hotel had a fairly nice restaurant, nice swimming pool and a rec room. I over-ate at the restaurant, so I did not feel like any activity afterwards. I went back up to my room and slept until five-thirty in the morning. I felt really rested, and was ready to go. I picked up the rest of my things in my suitcase and went downstairs to get their complimentary breakfast. I turned in my key at the desk, and walked into the dining area. As I sat down with my luggage, I saw four men in suits carrying large military style rifles rush up the stairway to the second floor. I did not like what I saw, so I grabbed several donuts and went outside. I went out into the parking lot, and hid behind a pickup truck. After a few minutes, the same men came out of the hotel and got into a black van. Their presence told me a lot. After they left, I boarded the bus. I kept my luggage with me, holding it in my lap. The bus was mostly empty so nothing was said when I placed my luggage on the seat beside me. At precisely seven o'clock, the bus roared out of the hotel parking lot and on to the road to San Antonio. It was a smooth, easy ride in the bus, compared to the Jeep ride I had in Mexico. There are advantages to leaving the driving up to them.

It seemed like we stopped at every little intersection that had a store of some type. Those were bus stops, so we had to at least come to a quick stop, then leave. Eventually, we made it to San Antonio. I had a good friend named General Coleman Cook that I had dealings with in a case years back, temporally stationed there. We kept in touch, and we went mountain climbing, and skiing together a time or two. When we pulled into the large bus station in San Antonio, I went to the pay phone and gave him a call. I had his direct line, so I did not need to go through his secretary.

"Hey Coleman, this is Zeb. I need to talk with you, in private. Can we meet somewhere?"

"Zeb? I saw reports that you were dead. It was on the news a little while back. I did not get any kind of funeral notification. I am really glad to hear those reports were not true."

"Coleman, the truth about me has to be kept quiet for now. Tell no one. Where can we meet?"

"Well, why don't I just pick you up where you are? How would that be? Then, we can go and get something to eat."

"Okay, great. Just be careful that no one follows you."

"Follows me? Okay, I will keep an eye out for something like that."

"I'm at the down town Greyhound bus station. When can you get here?"

"Well, I can leave right now; I have nothing but paperwork to do. I can leave any time. How about right now?"

"Great, I'll be waiting for you. What kind of car do you drive?"

"I have a new Crown Victoria, black in color. I know where you are at, so hang tight. I'll be there shortly."

I hung up the phone, and I felt that I had done the right thing by calling him. He had considerable power and influence. I could not have asked for a better friend. I sat back on one of the chairs in the bus lobby and watched out the front windows for a black Crown Victoria.

He arrived in twenty minutes, wearing his dress uniform, with four stars on his shoulders and his hat. He was an impressive person, tall, athletic, and intelligent. I needed his help. I put my suitcase in the back seat and got in the front seat of his car.

"Zeb, great to see you! Where would you like to go for a bite to eat?" He asked before putting his car back into gear.

"I don't know what's good around here. How about your choice! I said with a smile.

"Okay, you've got it. I know a great restaurant that serves good old-fashioned American food not too far from here. I've eaten there several times, and it's been great!"

"Okay, sounds good!" I said anticipating a good selection of things to eat, done up right. It took us about ten minutes to get there, and there were only a few places to park. I saw that as a good sign that the food was good. Bad food and bad service leaves a restaurant parking lot empty. We hurried on in and were brought immediately to a nice VIP table. We were warmly greeted and both given menus.

"Their steaks are to die for, my friend." He said from behind his menu.

"Well, that sounds mighty good. Everything really looks delicious."

"Only because it is." He said with a chuckle.

We both ordered steaks, stuffed baked potatoes and a side item of green beans. The meals were surprising brought in short order style.

"Well, now tell me what is going on with you, Zeb," Coleman said as we settled into our meals.

I warned him in advance that he may not like what he heard, but he waved me on. So, I didn't leave any detail out that was important. I finished telling him my story by the time we finished our deserts. He sat back and thought for a while after I was done.

"What you are telling me is news to me. I had no idea that the CIA acted in such a manner."

"Well, Coleman, word has it, through a friend of mine, Rick Hasselbon."

"Rick Hasselbon? Yes, I have met and talked with him several times. He seems like a levelheaded man. He works in the intelligent department..."

"He told me that it was the CIA that had the Kennedy's assassinated both of them. They also took Nixon out."

Coleman sat at the table expressionless. "I'm surprised that he said that. You know, people shouldn't be going around spreading wild rumors like that."

"I had heard before that it was the mafia that took the Kennedys out. Coleman, he only told me in confidence. He does not go around telling everybody everything he knows.

Another thing, if Rick said it, it is not a wild rumor. Like you said, he is level headed."

The general sat in his chair again for a minute without saying anything. "Does he have proof of what he told you?"

"I don't know, probably. I didn't ask him."

Coleman took a drink of his sweet tea, "So, if this is true, and I'm not saying that it is, then, I am going to look into it myself. Now, concerning the secret weapon...that is what the missing bridge is all about, isn't it?"

"Yes, it is all about some forbidden, secret nuclear weapon system."

"Well, it sounds like to me that this spinning missile that carries multiple warheads that are dirty bombs is illegal. They kill not just by an explosion, but also by the poison of the radiation. That kind of bomb is not held in our arsenals. It's illegal, and in violation of our international treaties."

"So, we don't have one of those anywhere?" I asked.

"No."

"Are you sure that some department somewhere doesn't have a secret development program that you don't know about?"

"I'm not one hundred percent sure of anything right now. I can look into it. Hold on," He waved for a waiter to bring a phone to the table.

"Senator Mark Collins, please." Coleman said to someone on the phone. "Zeb, he's my go to man when I have questions. He will either know or will find out."

"Mark, this is General Coleman Cook, I have a question for you. Have you ever heard of X Caliber X.? It is a secret project of the Pentagon. The CIA seems to have something to do with it."

"X Caliber X? No, I never heard of it. What is it?"

"A secret nuclear delivery system. It's basically a nation killer."

"No sir. I will check into it for you, right now. Let me call you right back." General Cook hung up the phone.

"He is going to call me right back," Coleman said, so we sat there and made small talk while we waited. We tentatively made plans to do some skiing next month in Switzerland. The phone rang. The general talked for just a minute, and then hung up with a frown on his face.

"Nothing! The Pentagon denies the existence of such a program, and the CIA claims to have never heard of it. Come on let us go back to the base. I can do some of my own research from there." The general graciously paid for both of our meals and we went back to the base.

I brought my suitcase with me. In his office, he made several phone calls. Later, a staff sergeant came in with several reports. General Cook carefully looked through all of them.

"Zeb, you are going to like this. It is here. We have this secret weapon in field storage. This base has four thousand acres and that thing is on one of them. He called for his personal attendant to bring a base vehicle around to the front. We got into the military vehicle and the driver took us to Zone Zero, which was sectioned off from the rest of the base by a heavy duty, high fence with electrical wiring interlaced through it. We stopped at the gate, and the guard opened it for us.

Upon driving in, we could see a large, long object covered with a grey thick tarp resting on a long trailer. There were warning signs all over the parameter to stay well back and not approach the object. We got out of the vehicle.

"Sergeant, what is under the tarp?" General Cook asked.

"Sir, I don't know. I am just a guard."

Have you seen what is under the tarp at any time?"

"No, sir."

General Cook walked back to the guard's station and called the Colonel who was in charge of Zone Zero. I walked back to the guard's station to listen to the conversation.

"You can't tell me what is stored in Zone Zero? Why is that? You know you are talking to General Cook." I could not hear the reply, but the general had a disgusted look on his face. "So, can we get a crew out here to take this tarp off so we can see what is underneath it?" he asked. "No? What do you mean no? What? You mean you are telling me that you have strict orders from the Pentagon to keep it secret until notified? I do not believe you are telling me that! How is it that I have been by-passed? A need to know, only? For whom? From Whom? What?" he stood there with his mouth gapping wide open, speechless for a moment, then he slammed the phone down. "Heads are going to roll!" he said and got back in the parked vehicle. "Come on, we're going back to my office!" He was not happy.

20.

A Far Out Expedition

WE WENT BACK TO GENERAL Cook's office where he made a series of phone calls, some not too pleasant. I waited patiently in his office for him to finish his calls in order to talk with him. He was definitely upset, but he calmed down after he made his calls.

"I'm going to Washington; I would like you to go with me." He said.

"Do you think that is wise? It seems like someone there wants me out of the way. It could be dangerous for the both of us."

"Don't worry, you will be with me," he said. "We will be talking to the Joint Chiefs of Staff at the Pentagon and one cabinet member. We are about to get this straightened out. Are you with me, Zeb? You can go as what's his name, Clyde Ryner."

"When do we leave, sir?"

"Now, they are pulling the jet out of the hanger even as we speak." I picked up my suitcase that I had left there in his office and we went out and got into his waiting vehicle. The driver took us to the airstrip and there was a small two engine, jet waiting for us. We got in and it took off heading east. I sat my suitcase down beside my seat. It was nice to have privileges like no waiting. On board, there were two nice flight attendants and two men in the pilot's compartment. We were the only other ones on board. They served us some sandwiches and drinks about half way through the flight. In Washington, we landed at the

Dulles International Airport[1]. There was a black limousine that took us from the airport to the Pentagon. I was given special guest status at the door via the general. They carefully examined the contents of my luggage, and then, let me continue carrying it. We walked back to a large meeting room that had a large mahogany desk and executive chairs. We sat down and waited as the Joint Chiefs of Staff filed in. Senator Mark Collins was one of the last to come in the room. Several members of the House Armed Service committee were present also. The chairman stood and spoke.

"We now call this meeting to order. We are here to squash any false rumors that seem to be circulating concerning a so-called secret military program called X Caliber Ten. We have done a thorough review of what we know has been circulated, and are here to categorically deny any such project exists. Not only does it not exist but also we have no plans for it to ever exist. The United States is not in the business of poisoning nations, friendly or otherwise. Furthermore, as Chairman, I speak for the President as well; we strictly forbid any member of this staff or any member of the military to spread any such detrimental rumor that would besmirch the integrity of this great nation. We are the defenders of freedom, upholding the value of human life. Therefore, any member of the military who spreads such non-truths will be dealt with severely. Now, gentlemen, I believe I've made myself clear. You are dismissed."

The staff stood at attention when he left the room, and then all filed quietly out.

"That's it?" I asked General Cook.

He looked over at Senator Collins. Senator Collins just shrugged his shoulders and left. He looked disgusted.

"So, that's the end of it," he said. "I can't argue against my superiors. I would lose my stars. Let's go." General Cook said.

---

1.   https://en.wikipedia.org/wiki/Dulles_International_Airport

We went back to the airport. We boarded the jet while it was still in the hanger. I kept my luggage in my lap. We had two pilots seated up front that were different from before, but I did not see any flight attendants. I greeted the pilots as I got myself situated with my suitcase. I noted that neither of them replied or acknowledge my presence, but continued with their take-off checklist. I thought that it was unusual that they just stayed to the front and did not acknowledge us at any time. The doors shut from the outside.

The warning lights flashed and we heard the announcement to fasten our seatbelts as we taxied down the runway. We took off without any delays or problems and it was the smoothest take-off that I had ever experienced. I never felt the plane rise, but I could clearly see out the window that we were taking off, and the engines were louder as we lifted into the sky. It continued to be a smooth flight for ten minutes. Then, something very strange appeared on both sides of the jet.

"General, look at this, what are those things?" I asked.

Two very large, solid black flying saucer shaped objects began flying parallel to the jet.

General Cook looked out of the jet windows, "I don't know what those are. I have never seen anything like it. Captain, can we out fly these things? Speed up, man!"

I could hear the jet engines get faster and louder and we rose in elevation. The two dark objects continued to fly in parallel with us. The general went to the front to look out the pilot's window. Now, not far in front of us was one huge, black flying saucer.

"What is that? Captain, take evasive action!" General Cook demanded. He looked down at the captain and co-pilot. Their seats were empty! "Zeb, did the captain just go by you?"

"No, sir, no one has come back here. They seem to have disappeared." I watched General Cook scramble to get into the pilot's seat. He was an accomplished pilot, but had difficulty getting into the seat. I went up to the pilot's compartment and saw a giant dark object just in front of the nose of our jet. Suddenly, a large door lifted open in front of us, and our jet glided into the dark interior of the saucer. The jet came to rest in a large empty room and the door shut behind us. Suddenly, it was dark. Our jet engines went out like a light. Coleman Cook and I were captives of whoever operated this machine. The lighting in the jet was still working, so we were not in the dark as long as we stayed inside. We examined six multi-colored lights above the pilot's seats that should not have been there.

"Well, here is something else I was not told about. I think I know what those are. Let us get out and see our captors. Do you have any weapons?"

"No, sir, just a pocket knife, and this suitcase."

"That's more than I have. Let's go." We both got the jet door open and climbed out. The floor was as solid as if we were on pavement.

"Come on, there's a door over there." The general pointed to a green door across the room. On the other side, we found a wall of blinking lights and switches. There was a small port like window to the right of the large control panel. We walked over and looked out. We could see a very illuminated earth thousands of miles away. The room had another door, so we tried it. It was secure. "Don't worry; I can get this thing open. Give me your knife."

I handed it to him and he worked it between the latches. In a few minutes, the door was open. We discovered that we were in an airport hangar.

"Whoa! This is something like what happened to me one other time. It is like a Hollywood production or something. I don't understand the use of the phony UFO," I said.

"I had no idea that they had developed this so far!" The general exclaimed.

"Developed what so far?"

"It's a new top secret science called Holographic Projection. I do know about that project. It is fantastic. That is how the pilot and attendants disappeared. They were never there. We never left the hangar or even took off.in this thing."

"So, none of that was real? Just the plane? It was just projections?"

"Basically, sort of like the Moon Landing."

"What about the moon landing?"

"Come on, Zeb, I guess you never noticed how that Neal Armstrong was semi-transparent on your TV screen while hopping around on the moon? The camera was just slowed down so that they looked to be jumping around weightless. You never heard about how they dropped the moon return capsule from a C-5A that was flying over the Pacific. It was all done to fulfill the impossible dream of JFK, and it saved us and the USSR millions. The USSR wanted out of the space race, and gave us a chance to save face with the American public. So, it was a win-win situation for both sides. They have carried the show on for years. None of this was real, never was. Now, forget I ever told you that. Let's get out of here."

We went to the Capital Building to the office of Senator Collins. He was in a meeting, so we decided to wait for him.

"So, you mean, our government has been lying to us about things?" I asked the general. "It is totally unbelievable."

"The news feeds you what they want you to believe. Life goes on."

"Yes, it goes on, but not the same," I said in disappointment.

"Oh, don't worry about it. It is for your own good. The higher ups deal with perception and deception, mostly to keep the peace and to save money. The money saved is just more money that can go into their bank accounts. I am not totally ignorant of everything that goes on, just some of it."

When the senator did come in, he was surprised to see us. "Come; let's go into my office, where we can talk."

We went in and told him what we had just experienced.

"Oh, senator, would you have your secretary make a dozen copies of my files for me right away?" I handed him my file of top-secret documents. "Have one made for yourself, sir."

" Sure, it will only take a few minutes. Sorry about what happened to you. There is nothing that I can do about any of it, not even as a senator." He handed my paper work to his secretary and she copied the documents while we stood there. She put them in their own folders and handed them all back to me. The senator put his copy on his desk. The phone rang and after the senator hung up, he said, "Mr. Dasher, you have someone here who wants to see you. You may leave now, if you would like. He is waiting for you out in the hall. I have another meeting to go to. Thank you."

"Thank you Senator," we both shook the senator's hand and left his office. Out in the hall, we found Rick Hasselbon standing there waiting.

Zeb! Hello General Cook, nice to see you." He shook both of our hands and we walked together down the hall. During the conversation, General Cook told us that he was going to fly back to Texas. Rick and I decided that it would be best to go back to Youngstown. He said that he would help me write up a report. He told me that he knew some details that I did not know. I wanted a complete report so that I could close my case to my own satisfaction. He drove us non-stop back to Youngstown that day, and I was tired by the time we pulled into his driveway. I still had an uncertain feeling about Rick, but at the time, helpful friends were hard to come by. I hope that that is what he was.

We settled in for the evening. I got my pajamas out of my luggage and got ready for bed. I took the sofa and he went to bed. In the middle of the night Rick talking on the telephone awakened me. He kept his voice down, and rather muffled. I could not tell what he was talking about, but it disturbed me so much that I had trouble going back to sleep. I got up off my floor bed around five thirty, not well rested. I took all my important paper work and put it into my suitcase. Then I quietly carried my suitcase outside and hid it behind the last large tree in the driveway. I took all but one copy of my top-secret files and stuffed them under my shirt. The suitcase was well hidden by the bushes that grew around the tree. It was a better quality suitcase that was supposed to be water resistant, so I was fairly sure my things would be safe there. I quietly went back inside and sat down on the sofa. Rick came out of his bedroom shortly after that. He whipped together some bacon and eggs for our breakfast, and we sat down to eat and talk.

"So, when do you want to get started on the report? I would like to turn it in to the Clarion City Council as soon as possible, and close this case. They still owe me twenty five thousand dollars. I don't get paid until I turn in the report."

"Oh, that. Well, you can start on it anytime that you want to, Zeb."

"So, who were you talking to in the middle of the night?" I asked.

"Let's finish up our meal, and then we will talk about it." He replied.

I helped him clean up the skillet and dishes. Afterwards we sat down again at the table to talk.

"Well, Zeb, old friend, I hate that I have to tell you this. You will not be collecting twenty five thousand dollars from the Clarion City Council."

"Why not?"

"The official story has now been published. It was all a hoax perpetrated by the city council. The hoax was to bring in tourists to the area. It was a money thing. There's even pictures of the bridge being recovered out to the water in the newspaper, see."

He handed a Clarion newspaper to me and there it was in black and white. There were several pictures of eyewitnesses, also. "The Clarion mayor has apologized in a press conference, and there are a lot of law suits going around. So, there you go, no twenty five thousand dollars because those council members aren't there anymore. They are gone. The official story just saved the city twenty five thousand dollars, and you are not needed."

"What a cover-up! They may be gone but I still have a legally binding contract."

"It's not going to hold up in court. All those people have all moved to Minnesota and are unavailable to testify."

"Minnesota? What are all of them doing up there?"

"I don't know, Zeb. Maybe you could ask the armed men standing outside the door," he said with a slight smile. "Sorry, old pal, it was either you or me, so there you go."

21.

Saving the Environment

"SIR, IF YOU WILL STEP outside with your hands up, things will go better for you." One of the men outside said. There were two men standing in the doorway with raised guns trained on me.

"Can I ask what this is all about?"

"I think you know."

I raised my hands and walked to the door. "No, I don't know."

"All I can tell you is where you will be going. Now step to the car." They put my hands behind my back and handcuffed me. "You have to catch a plane flight." They tucked me into the back seat of the police cruiser, and locked the door. I did not like the thought of another government sponsored plane flight. All those files that I had stuck into my pants were very uncomfortable. I worried that the government agents may spot them.

"A flight to where?" I asked through the door window glass.

"Minnesota."

"There's that state again. What is in Minnesota?

"A fertilizer plant that you are going to take a close look at. Just consider it an inspection of what they are producing, Detective Dasher. I think it's something that you will really get into," he said and the two men chuckled. They turned on the revolving blue lights on the roof, and then took me to the Akron Airport. I was loaded into a cargo plane with twelve other people who also were in restraints. I wondered what the government had against all of those people. They were dressed in various ways. One was in a hospital gown. A young woman was dressed as if she were about to go dancing. A man was in his pajamas, and another was in his underwear. One man was just in a bath towel. A man and a woman were in their swimming suits. We sat on metal fold-up benches that were built into the walls of the plane's interior. Without delay, we were up in the sky and on our way to some place in Minnesota.

The older man that sat beside me asked, "Do you know what is going to become of us?"

"No, not for sure, but I think from all the hints, we are about to become fertilizer." I replied.

"Fertilizer!" the man exclaimed, and then he wept uncontrollably.

"You, over there, shut up!" the guard yelled, then walked away.

The young attractive woman on the other side of me leaned over and whispered. "Hey, I can get us out of these cuffs. I know how. I pick locks for a living. They got me here for breaking into a secret government office that stored classified documents. I could have made millions had I not been caught. Now, the only ones who will get rich are the crooked politicians who will secretly sell that stuff to the highest bidder. I get turned into fertilizer, and they get rich. Now, are you with me if I release you? There is only one guard back here. We can jump him, and get his side arm."

"One hundred percent." I whispered back. The young woman began moving her hands around, and then, she quietly reached over and did something to the cuffs on my wrists. I felt the cuffs release. "Let's get him over here." I whispered. The young woman put the small wire that she used to unlock the cuffs under her right leg, and then pretended to be still cuffed.

"Sir, sir! Can I ask you a question? It's kind of personal." The young woman said and smiled.

The guard stood there for a moment, and then went over to the young woman. He leaned over and asked with a smile, "What is it?"

"This!" I said as my right fist crashed to the back of his neck. His helmet fell off, and he collapsed limply to the floor. "Come on; let's get everyone out of their cuffs in a hurry!" The young woman began releasing one prisoner at a time, as I looked for the keys on the guard. Once I had them, everyone was freed quickly.

"Now, what?" someone asked.

"Can anyone fly this plane?"

"I was in the air force for ten years, and have flown a plane like this many times," a middle-aged man replied.

We quietly went to the front of the plane. There were two pilots and a third man in the cockpit.

"Kind of a light load this time around, isn't it Bret?" the pilot asked the co-pilot.

"From what I understand, there's another flight coming from the west coast that is loaded to capacity. After they get rid of the right wing riff-raff, they will soon be able to consolidate California and Washington."

The third man asked, "Who are they neutralizing out there?"

"I think they are working all the major systems, the university professors, key politicians, scientists and medical men. If they are an undesirable, then, they get one of our free one-way rides. They just disappear, with some official fake story is given in the newspapers. Car accidents are big, ands suicides are on the increase. Many empty closed caskets are being buried. "

"Lawn Nutrient Fertilizer is a secret operation run by the CIA. They oversee all of this with the co-operation of the EPA," the co-pilot said to the third man. "It's good for the environment, you know. Less people, less waste. We are lucky to get spots on the program. Pay for each of these flights is better than piloting a passenger airline."

"Makes sense to me, I'm all for saving planet earth, and getting paid at the same time," the third man said.

"The whole thing is to get rid of the opposition and their undesirable ideas. After they are gone, we control everything. We can then go on to dominate the world with our new secret weapons. There are over fifty of them already deployed in the northern states. From what I understand, they almost lost one of them. It was dumped in a river somewhere, but has been moved to Texas for repair. I'm just glad that I'm part of the team," The pilot said.

"Yes, I like being on the winning side. Wow, I hadn't heard about any new weapons," replied the co-pilot with an anxious expression on his face. "What do you know about them? I mean, what are they?"

"I don't know much, it's all very hush-hush. They cannot just let anyone know about what is going on. I do know that they have a nation killer that if released, could be even a continent killer. It is just that powerful. No one would stand a chance against it. It is designed with two new ultra, supersonic rocket engines that would make it just about impossible to knock down. Not even the X-15 could catch it."

"Wow that is amazing. Anything else?"

"Yes, get out of those seats," I said as I forcefully laid my hands on the shoulders of the pilot. A large man to my right did the same to the co-pilot. We forcefully lifted them out of their positions, and then, took all three of them to the back. They were cuffed and then tied to their seats with some rope that was found. Two former passengers got into the pilot seats and took over the controls. I took my files and tucked them into a bag, which fit, under my shirt. My shirt was my only hiding place. At least now, they did not shift around so much or bother me. If I was inspected, those would be easily found, but that may not happen.

"What's next?" someone asked.

"What's the flight plan?" I asked.

"We are headed to central Minnesota right now," came the reply from our new pilot.

"I'm afraid if we deviate from our course, they will know something has happened." I said. "See if the guard's uniform fits anyone here, and what about the pilot's outfit? Can anyone get into it? We will fake our way out of this when we touch down."

There was a frenzy of people grabbing the clothing and seeing if it fit... Three men fit into the pilot's uniforms. One man was able to get into the guard uniform fairly well. It was not a perfect fit, but close. Within twenty minutes, we were circling a Minnesota airport. Our captives had rags stuffed in their mouths. Those of us who were not in uniforms had to wear handcuffs. We made sure that the handcuffs were placed on our wrists loose enough that we could slip out of them when the time came.

We touched down, shortly and were directed to a short runway that led to a drop off point. There was a bus waiting there that had "State Prisoners" painted in large letters on the sides. The three men dressed as pilots were given copies of my secret files, and they walked off to their freedom. The rest of us were ushered onto the security bus. From there we were transported out of town to a remote factory that had high voltage, electrical fencing around it. The bus stopped at the gate and then proceeded to a central receiving and processing center. We exited the bus and were taken single file into a large room that had a glass wall that displayed the factory. The original pilots of the plane started to struggle, but they were carried directly to the front of the line.

As we waited, I watched through the glass naked people going into a double green door on the opposite side of the room they were in. The door was reopened a few minutes later, and the people that had entered were never seen again. I knew then that this was the destiny of the state's opposition. Now, we had seen enough, it was time to act.

We were still all together. I yelled, "Now!" and everyone slipped their cuffs off. I pulled my gun out and yelled, "Everyone on the floor!" I waved the gun around and the guards got down on the floor. "Get their guns! Cuff them!" I shouted.

There was no resistance, and we were able to get everyone who was in line out and packed into the state prisoner bus in a hurry. One man grabbed the driver's keys and put on the driver's hat. Everyone knelt on the floor so as to not be seen, and we drove to the gate. The alarm had not gone off yet. The men at the gate opened it, and the bus was driven straight out of there to freedom.

The driver yelled, "We better ditch this bus, and scatter, or they are going to get us all."

We rode to a small roadside convenience store and parked the bus in the back. Everyone got out and went into the store, dressed the way they were. Some people still had money; some used the phones there to call loved ones to pick them up. Some left, walking away into the fields away from the roads. Two cars parked on the side of the building were hot-wired and taken. I gave four copies of my secret files to people I thought who would use them. One was a newscaster from Chicago, another was a newspaper publisher from California. Then other person was a prominent lawyer from New York City and the last one to get a copy of my files was a well-known politician from Texas. I was hoping that someone would be able to get the word out of what was going on. I watched the two cars carrying those people with the files disappear down the road. The cars were packed, and I decided to let them escape. I would find my way out of here, or my name is not Zeb Dasher.

22.

Saving the Nation

I went back into the convenience store and asked the old man behind the counter to use his phone. The store was a mom and pop operation, sort of off the beaten path. The only customers that they usually had were from the fertilizer plant.

"What do you know about the factory down the road?"

"Nothing really. I think they use a lot of labor from the prisons. I see the state prison buses go by four or five times a day. I suppose that keeps costs down."

"Have you ever went out there and visited the factory?"

"No sir, I haven't. I have never even been past it. I live in the opposite direction."

"Let me speak with General Cook, please," I said to a woman on the other end of the phone line. I had dialed the general's direct number and expected to speak to the general. The secretary never answered his personal phone.

"Sorry, the general is not here. He went to Washington, D.C. several days ago, and has not made it back yet. I haven't heard from him."

I hung up the phone, and was fearful for the general's life. I decided to call his D.C. office. The phone rang but was never answered. I called his home number in Texas and his wife answered the phone.

"Yes, Detective Dasher, he is here, but we are getting ready to go to the mountains for a while. Would you like to talk to him?"

"Yes, I would," I replied. I waited a minute for him to come to the phone.

"Zeb? Where are you? I've been expecting to hear from you." General Cook said.

"I'm in Minnesota, just a few miles down the road from the Lawn Nutrient Fertilizer factory. You will not believe what I have been through. I was in line to be made into fertilizer, Coleman!"

"Fertilizer! You must be joking, Zeb. I never heard of such a thing."

"It's not just me, but all sorts of people are being run through there. Probably thousands a day."

"Thousands? Zeb, you are talking out of your mind. Are you on some sort of prescription medication, Zeb?"

"No sir. You must believe me. I need your help. It is all tied to the secret weapon stored on your base. There is more than just that one. They have around fifty of them in northern states, sir."

"Fifty? I would think that I would have been notified about at least some of this since they are using my base. I just don't understand why I'm out of the loop."

"Well, sir, it's probably your political views. You are not on their side of the political tracks. From what I can see, they are gradually purging people like you from the military. It's not just the military, sir; it's everywhere, every institution, and every agency of government."

"Zeb, you sound like another McCarthy. You remember Senator McCarthy from the fifties. He was finding communists everywhere. He was nuts."

"I know what I sound like, and I know it's unbelievable, but listen. I need to get out of here. I am at the Mom and Pop General Store close to the fertilizer factory. Can you come and pick me up, or have me picked up? I need a way out of here."

"Okay, Zeb. We are on our way to a retreat in Canada. I suppose we could pick you up. It will be a little out of our way, but not too very bad. I can do that for a friend. Okay, we will be leaving here, shortly. Just stay where you are, and my wife and I will pick you up today."

"Okay, I'll be waiting. Thank You," I hung up. The old man behind the counter took the phone back.

"I couldn't help but hearing what you were saying on the phone, young man. You mean to tell me that they are processing humans into fertilizer out there? Isn't that against the law?"

They are, and yes, it is. Now, for your own good, do not let anyone know that you know about what is going on. If you do, your life may be in danger."

"You bet, sonny. Mum is the word. Those must be some kind of Nazi's running that place. You know they were gassing and burning people in Europe some years ago. People that they didn't like or fit in, they were killed and put in mass graves."

"Well, here, they don't even get that. They are ground up and mixed with other things. Then they are scattered to the wind."

"So, you are being picked up? You can wait in the back room until then. You don't need to be out front, here, if someone comes in."

"Thank you sir. I appreciate that." I replied.

The old man walked to a closed door behind the counter, and unlocked it.

"Here you go. There's a back door that you can go out on the other side if you need to," He said and waved me in with a nod.

I paid for a bag of chips, a sandwich and a drink before I went to the back room. Once I was in the room, I found that the back door had been locked so I would not be able to get out that way if I needed. There was a refrigerator, table and chair and a floor lamp in the room. I turned to tell the old man that the back door would not open, when the door that I had entered slammed shut. I heard the door being locked from the outside. I was once again a prisoner. If I could not get out, then it was up to those to whom I had given my secret files to release the information to the public and save the nation. If they did not do that, and I would be turned into dust, all would be lost!

23.

The Deep Sleep

I pounded on the door and shouted to the old man, but there was no response. The door was secure, so there was no getting out that way. I decided to check the back door again. It was locked. I found a wire clothes hanger tried to shape it similarly, to what I remembered the wire the young woman had who set me free. I had nothing to cut the wire with so I bent it back and forth until it finally broke. Then, I took the wire and placed it in the back door lock. Moving it around in the lock, I hoped to be able to unlock it. It was an old lock so it was probably simple. I stood there for hours with no success, then suddenly, I heard the front door unlock. It did not open. I did not want to go out the front door since it easily could be a trap, but actually, I had no choice.

Cautiously, I pushed the door open and looked around. The storefront looked empty. I didn't see the old man anywhere, but who opened the door? I stepped out and was grabbed from behind. A rag was placed over my mouth and nose, and I was out. I went into a deep sleep.

Sometime later, I woke up strapped down on what appeared to be a kitchen table. The room was barren except for some wall cabinets. A large round light hung just above me. There was no one else in the room. The straps were pretty firm but I managed to start moving downward under the straps. I gradually worked my way out from under them and slid off the bottom of the table without it tipping over.

I next opened the unlocked door, and found that curtains covered the front of the door on the other side. It opened into the storefront. I was glad that I was still at the store. I could hear two men talking to each other outside. Quietly, I moved to the storefront window and looked out. There were two men dressed in green standing under the storefront awning. There was a matching green box van at the gas pumps. I looked around and found a baseball bat that I could use as a weapon. It would not be much if those men had guns. I order to avoid the confrontation, and possible re-capture, I looked behind the store counter for keys. On a shelf below the single drawers that lined the bottom of the counter, I found a set of keys. I quickly took the keys and went to the back door. One of them unlocked the door!

Anxiously, I made my way outside. Cautiously looking around, I closed the door behind me. There were some bushes and trees a few yards away on the other side of the dumpster. I decided that I should hide there for a while until the general arrived. Once I was hidden, I had time to think. I wondered if I had missed him. I could have been knocked out and strapped down when he came through here. I was not sure why my captures had not just thrown me into the back of the van and hauled me off to the processing plant. That question was shortly answered when the two men from the front walked around the store to the back. They stood there and casually looked around, and began talking to each other again. Apparently, they were unaware that I had escaped.

"The Big Man wants this dude, personally, you know, back in DC. I guess he's a special thorn in the flesh to him or something." One of them said.

"Well, he apparently is classified as a national security threat. So, all we have to do is keep him on ice until they pick him up."

"I hope they give us a reward for capturing him. They do that with criminals, you know," the one man chuckled.

"Right, maybe, we will get the medal of freedom from the President or something. After all, we are saving our democracy from our enemies."

Just then, I heard a car pull up out front.

"Maybe, that's the transport now,"

The two men went around the building, so I came out of my hiding place. I circled around the other side of the building and saw that a Lincoln Town Car had pulled up. It was the general and his wife.

The two men in green went over to the car, "Sorry, sir, the proprietor has stepped out for a bit. There's no one here to sell you any gasoline."

The general got out of the car. He was in his civilian clothing. He was not a small man at six feet six, and at two hundred and seventy five pounds. He dwarfed the two men in green.

Have you seen a man around here, probably dressed in a suit, about six feet tall, crew cut, muscular, thirty or maybe forty? He is not from around here. He is lost. Have you seen him by some chance?"

"No," the two men in green answered in unison.

"I'm going to take a look around. If you don't work here, why are you here, standing around?"

"We are waiting on someone from the home office. We are to meet him here."

"I see, well, if you will excuse me, I won't be long."

"Oh, there's no one inside. We were just in there, so there is no need to even bother going in. It is just us. There's no one else around." One of the men in green stated.

"Thanks, but I'm going to look around anyway. It's what I do."

The general left his wife waiting in the car with the motor running, while he went inside. The two men in green followed him in, right behind him.

"Thanks, but I don't need any help." The general said.

"We will go along so that no one can say that you stole anything," one of them said.

"Do you see that nice new Lincoln? I just bought it, and paid cash for it. So, no, I'm not coming into this store to steal something." The general walked around behind the counter and looked into the room where I had been locked up as a prisoner. Then he circled around to the curtain and found the door behind it. He opened it and saw the table with the straps still on it. "I wonder what that is used for," he walked past the door and went to the front window. The two men in green looked in at the empty table and panicked.

"What are we going to tell the Big Guy?" one asked.

"He has to be here somewhere," the other replied.

The general standing at the storefront window watched me sneak over to his car and get in the back seat. That was all he needed to see.

"Well, I'm satisfied that he's not here. So, I hope you have a nice meeting with your boss."

General Cook went and got into his car and we drove off. I looked behind as we drove away, and I could see the two men going around the parameter of the store looking for me. I was glad I was out of there.

"We are going to take the back roads to Canada. You know, I think that you may be right about things, as wild as they sound. We may be dealing with a government within the government. That is why I have been left out of the loop of things. Someone in my position is not usually left out of important projects, especially if it involves the base that is assigned to them.

"So, we have maybe been taken over by a cabal, maybe a cabal of NAZI's or Communists?" I asked.

"Maybe. Right now things do not fit together right. It will take time to figure out. I'm not the kind of man who jumps to conclusions." The general said.

"But, dear, what were you telling me about the fertilizer plant? That is about as un-American as it can get. Don't you think?" Emily asked.

"Yes, Emily, you are absolutely right about that. The American public is held in the dark concerning that, and all of their covert operations. What it sounds like they are doing is that they are taking over the entire country little by little, one section at a time, state by state, institution by institution. It has to be a long term plan."

"Yes, but Coleman, I've never heard of a lot of people disappearing, like you have told me. Thousands a day, you said? That is hard to believe." Emily said.

"It has to be disguised as deaths of various kinds." Coleman said.

"What about us, Coleman. I am scared. We aren't safe anymore,' Emily said holding back her tears.

"Mrs. Cook, don't worry. Knowledge is power. If we know what is going on, we can take proper safeguards. We aren't sitting ducks like the American population is." I said.

"So, the Pentagon has been taken over? If that is true, then that means there are other departments and branches of government that have likewise been compromised," the general said.

"I don't think the congress has not been taken over, at least not yet." I replied.

"Congress is made up of a bunch of do-nothings. They are just a political show. For sure, the CIA would be the cabal's think tank, This stuff is so far out, that maybe we are just imagining it all, like we are trapped in some sort of dream," Colemen said.

"Twilight Zone sort of stuff, Coleman, Twilight Zone!" Emily replied.

"Yes, but is always appears darkest before the dawn," I stated.

"If what we think is correct, then, it's pretty dark. What is that, up ahead? Is that a road block?" Coleman asked.

24.

The Darkness before the Dawn

"DO YOU STILL HAVE YOUR phony ID?" the general asked me. "You told me you had one."

I fumbled around in my wallet, and thankfully, it was still there. "Yes, yes, I do!"

"Great, we should be okay with the road block. Put my military hat and jacket on that's back there beside you." Coleman said. "Quickly."

I hurriedly did as he said and readied my ID in case I was asked for it. We pulled up to the state police car that was parked in the middle of the road. The state trooper came to Coleman's window.

"Hello. May I see your driver's license, insurance card and state registration, please?" he asked through the open window.

"I have a driver's license, a new temporary insurance card and the paperwork that shows the car registration has been applied for. I just bought this car, so I do not have the official registration yet. It is supposed to come in the mail in two or three weeks." Coleman said and handed the trooper the information through the window.

The trooper looked at it, and said, "Just a minute, sir, I have to call this in." He went back to his car. We sat there a good fifteen minutes before he came back to Coleman's window. "Sorry, but I have to ask you to step out of the car, please sir."

"For what?"

"Just get out of the car, unless you are attempting to interfere with my official duties. Let me advise you that I can arrest you for that."

"Alright, I'll get out, even though I don't know why." Coleman got out.

"Yes, sir, now open the trunk."

The general opened the trunk for the trooper. There was nothing more than luggage back there with our clothes in it.

"Open the suitcases."

Coleman opened the suitcases, and the trooper leafed through them. "You can close them now. Wait here."

The general stood there at the back of the car for quite a while. The trooper got out of his car and walked back up to the general.

"Who else is in the car?

"Just my wife and a friend."

"Who's your friend?"

"Clyde Ryner."

"Clyde Ryner? Okay, here is your driver's license back and your paperwork. You may go. I hope you have a safe day. Thank You," the trooper said. He went back to his patrol car and waited for the next car to show up. Coleman walked back to the Lincoln and got in the driver's seat.

"There's a one lane dirt road up ahead, on the right that goes right into Canada." The general said, as we started down the road, again.

"We've been down that way several times," Emily said. "Aren't you worried, Coleman? I mean, the federal government is looking for your friend. That makes you to be aiding and abetting a fugitive."

"Well, Honey, if I am, I am. We have wisely saved, so, even if I was fired, we would be okay."

We made a turn off to the right on a narrow, bumpy single lane road. The entrance to the small road was becoming overgrown with weeds and bushes, so a person could drive right by it and not even see it.

"How far is it?" I asked feeling the deep bumps in the road.

"About ten miles. It will take us a while because of this road. They rarely ever come through and maintain it. It seems like they forgot that it is here."

We slowly crossed a narrow, one lane wood bridge that looked to have been built in the last century. After that, I sat in the back until we eventually came out at the end of the dirt road to a different paved road.

"We are in Canada, now, Zeb. You can relax. We are almost to where we are going."

Nestled in the wood laden hills was a large white house with around a dozen small cabins located behind it. This was our Canadian destination. The Cook family came to this spot several times a year. It was Emily's favorite place. She had a cabin picked out that they stayed in each time they visited the retreat. Her cabin was located on the highest reach of the hill behind the main house. I was given the cabin just beneath it as my place to stay. Coleman had a month off and longer if he chose. I was not sure that I wanted to stay there that long. It was a very nice place, and the cabins were built with luxury to satisfy the whims of the rich who visited there. We could have stayed in the main house if we preferred that, but the Colemans liked the privacy of the cabins. Even though we stayed in the cabins, we could still enjoy meals in the main house. They had an excellent chef, and staff. There were also things to do in the main white house, besides eat. They had several game rooms including a bowling alley, and an indoor swimming pool. It was not much of a roughing it type place that I imagined it could have been. The stay there left no room for complaining.

The first month rolled into the second month. I wondered how things were going back in the states until I saw on the television newscast about the fertilizer plant in Minnesota exploding. It was the Nutrient Fertilizer processing plant with which I was all too familiar.

It was totally destroyed and would not be rebuilt. I went to Coleman's cabin to tell him about it.

Coleman opened the door, and I said, "Hey, have you heard, they blew up the fertilizer plant in Minnesota."

"I just saw that on the news, also. I wonder what really happened." He said and invited me into the cabin. Emily was making some cookies in the kitchen area, and the cabin smelled delicious.

"Could it be that the truth has leaked out, and they destroyed the evidence?" I asked.

"It very well could be. If that is true, we may see some changes being made to further cover it all up." The general said.

"You are right. It would make sense that they would slam a lid down on it, good and hard. The people of America may never know what is going on." I said. "Darkness covers the continent." I said.

"That is true. I suspect however, the silent purge of the opposition will continue but in a different manner. They will just keep going until they have total control."

"That will be impossible to find out in what manner they are operating, unless we can pry open CIA files in DC." I replied.

The senator may be able to help with that, somewhat." The general said.

"Senator Mark Collins? I wonder how much he knows. "He may be compromised also, since he is an acquaintance of Rick Hasselbon. Hasselbon stabbed me in the back, you know."

"He may not have had a choice." Coleman said. "It will do you no good to go to Washington, D.C. It would be like turning yourself in. If you will just stay here, Emily and I will go to DC. I will meet with Collins and see what I can come up with. I will call you from there and let you know."

"Rick may not have had a choice. He said it was either him or me. So, I suppose I should factor that in. They must threaten everyone they need to manipulate. They probably do this to members of congress, judges, and probably people in the executive branch." I said.

"Emily and I will make arrangements to leave tomorrow. In the meantime, let us enjoy what is left of our stay. How about a game of tennis? Are you up to it?"

"Sure, but I haven't played in years. So, go easy on me."

The general of course beat me in two games out of three, then he played his wife and lost. I am not sure if he let her win or maybe he was just tired at that point. Afterwards we had a snack and went to the swimming pool to relax. We mostly sat in the lounge chairs and sipped on sweet tea. There were only a few people who dove in and swam, so we watched them.

"I feel tired just watching them." Emily said.

"Well, we aren't teenagers any longer. It would be nice to be in our twenties again, though." Coleman said as if reflecting back to by-gone days.

"I'm satisfied with the way I am. I don't need to be any younger," I said to be different.

We finished the day with a nice meal in the dining room of the main lodge, and then retired to our separate cabins for the evening. Tomorrow, the general would leave in the morning to go to Washington, D.C. I hoped he would be able come up with some good news for a change. Staying at the cabin was nice, but I yearned to be back doing my job as Zeb Dasher. For that to happen, we needed to have some light shed on all the darkness of secrecy while being secretive ourselves. I wondered if that was even possible.

25

The Realization

THE NEXT DAY, I REMAINED in Canada and waited for a phone call from the general. Late in the afternoon, it came.

'Zeb? This is Coleman. I just had a private meeting with Senator Mark Collins at his apartment. It's not good."

"What isn't good, Coleman?" I asked.

"The whole situation stinks. It seems that the senator has very few people that he can rely on. He has a good staff, but the bureaucratic state of the centralized government is not cooperating with any of his inquiries. They are stonewalling him so far on certain things."

"Certain things?"

"He wasn't any more specific, Zeb. Oh, by the way, I talked to Rick Hasselbon.".

"What about? Talk about not being trusted. He's not reliable, I don't think."

"He is what he is, I guess. He called me, concerned about you."

"Oh, what a phony! He's the one who had me shipped off to the fertilizer factory, remember?" I said.

"He said that couldn't be helped. He was glad to hear that you were still alive."

"You didn't tell him that did you? Well, I guess who ever is after me already knows that. So, no damage done, but you didn't tell him where I was staying did you?" I said.

"No, absolutely not. I think that we are at a point that we must stick together on this thing, and not divulge any information about what we think, know and are planning to anyone. That anyone includes family. So, speaking of plans, what is next? What can we do? It seems like the bureaucracy runs the government, not the elected officials. Senator Collins seems helpless. I can't seem to get any cooperation at the Pentagon, and so I'll just stay clear of it for now," the general said.

"You know who may be able to help me? The police chief in Pittsburgh. He has been helpful before on things. He spent some time in the DC Intel network before becoming a police officer. He may be more reliable than Rick."

"Rick is what he is. He is somehow compromised as you have said. They have some sort of hold over him. He's good, but only to certain point."

"Right. When will you be back here?" I asked.

"Well, I have a few things to finish up on here, before I leave. I will see you soon enough. Hang in there. I will be in contact with you, bye."

"Okay, thanks, Coleman, and be careful." I hung up. I then decided to call Arnt Sigworth in Pittsburgh. He may be my best option.

The phone rang and Arnt picked up it up. "Hello, Chief Sigworth. How may I help you?" He sounded rushed.

"Arnt? Zeb Dasher. I need some help."

"Zeb Dasher! I heard you were dead! If you are still talking while dead, you do need help."

"I am Zeb Dasher. Remember ole Clinkenstein, your old boss? Don't be a jokester like him."

"Yeah, he was a real joke, so Zeb, what can I do for you?"

"Do you have much pull in any of the DC Intel groups these days?"

"Some, so what's up? What do you need to know?"

"Who's behind the top secret X Caliber Ten project?"

"X Caliber Ten Project? I never heard of it. What is it?"

"It's a secret nation killing weapon that is illegal. It has somehow found its way into our arsenal. I need to know who in DC and elsewhere is pushing it?"

"We are asking for nothing aren't we? I mean, if its top secret, then, that sounds pretty confidential. I will probably get nowhere with something top secret. They just don't hand that information out to anyone in brochures, you know."

"You used to have pretty high clearance in DC didn't you?" I asked.

"While I worked there, yes, all the way to the top, but I don't work there any longer. I still have contacts there though that do have top clearance. I'll see what I can come up with through them."

"Good enough. One thing, I do not know if you are aware of it, and this may sound a little nutty, but we are looking at the idea that we may be dealing with a shadow government in DC. I think it consists of mostly the bureaucrats. They actually write the laws and the congress and President signs off on them. It seems like that group has the CIA, FBI, and the Pentagon in their back pockets. I am not sure of this, so that is what I am now investigating. There may even be someone over them that I cannot name right now. Maybe you can help. They are somehow linked to the secret project."

"I'll do what I can, Zeb. It sounds as crazy as it is serious. A shadow government that is the real power? That is pretty deep, Zeb. I may lose all credibility looking into something like that."

"Please let me know as soon as possible on anything that you find out. Lives actually may depend on it, as well as our future liberty."

"I hope not. Okay Zeb. Only because it is you that is asking will I do such a thing. I think we are wasting our time though."

"Thanks Arnt. Maybe when this is all over, we can get together for some deer hunting. You still do that don't you?"

"Yes, but it's not in season right now. I'll let you know."

"Okay, I'll be looking forward to hearing from you and thanks again." I hung up the phone and turned on the television. The world news was on.

"Breaking, we have just received a report out of Washington, D.C. that the well-known and respected senator from Pennsylvania, Senator Mark Collins, has been found dead in his apartment. It is an apparent suicide...Police report that he suffered from a gunshot to the back of the head. A typed suicide letter was found on a table. There are no plans to investigate his death...."

Suicide? Mark would never commit suicide. He had too much going for him. He loved his family and his country too much to do that to himself. I then realized that Mark had not committed suicide at all but had been murdered. There did not seem to be any question by the police that it was suicide because they said that there was a typed good-bye letter signed by Mark found on his table. It didn't sound like Mark at all, so it wasn't. I could not accept such a conclusion. No investigation? I never realized it until now just how big this bridge case had become.

26

Looking for the Source

` "ZEB, LIVERMORE AND Los Alamos are the two possible places of origin for the warhead. The home base for these things is the Warren Air Force Base in Wyoming; however, it looks like the missiles in question were to be secretly deployed in several northern states. There are two versions of this weapon, the X Caliber Ten and the Peacemaker." Police chief Arnt said.

"Wow, Arnt, this is great information! What else do you have?"

"That's about it, Zeb. I am surprised that I was able to get that much. So, yes this secret weapon does exist. I never thought I'd be saying such a thing."

"Okay, all of that is good info, but just who is behind the financing of the development and distribution of illegal weapons? It is the who is behind it all question that now is the important thing. How to they pull the strings to do such things as this?" I asked.

"So you think that there's perhaps someone, a group of people, or groups of people working together doing this, but as of yet, it isn't known. So, then you still believe that there is a shadow government, unknown to the rest of us. Is that right Zeb?" Arnt asked.

"It looks like it's a good possibility. Did you hear about the death of Senator Collins?"

"Yes, I did. That is too bad. He was a good man. I just cannot understand him taking the suicide way out. It isn't like him at all."

"Exactly. He was looking into all this mess, also. Someone had him eliminated."

"Someone in the shadow government? Not all of this is something I deal with, or even want to deal with, Zeb. I'll let you deal with it if you want."

"Arnt, there has to be someone who controls the shadow government. There has to be a head giving direction. It's one man or one group of men, chief."

"Well, Zeb, I'll believe that one when you can prove that one."

"Arnt, remember, you didn't believe me about the secret weapon. So, it is just part of the big picture."

"Okay, right, keep me posted, Zeb. Come see me if you get to Pittsburgh sometime. I need to get going on some important things here, Zeb. Good-bye and good luck."

"Okay, and thanks again for your research. I may need to ask you again for information, but maybe not. Good-bye, and be careful." I hung up the phone.

I needed to find the string puller. Los Alamos may be a good place to start with that. Surely, someone there may know who gave the authorization for an illegal weapons development and deployment. I knew that here had to be a paper trail, and it could most naturally go through Los Alamos. For this, I may need the help of General Cook once again. I gave him a call.

"Coleman, Zeb here. When are you going to be back here? I have a new project that we need to be able to do together."

"I'm leaving for the airport now. I should be there in a few hours. What do you have in mind?"

"We need to go to the source of the weapons problem in order to find out who is in charge of it. In order to stop the plans of a rogue shadow government we need to find it first. Los Alamos is a good place to look. There has to be some sort of paper trail."

"Good thinking. And if there isn't a paper trail or a shadow government, we are wasting our time, Zeb. I think that idea is just a jump too far. We are probably just dealing with some top secret weapon's project that few know about." General Cook said.

"Yes, but an illegal one? Come on, we aren't a terrorist nation, are we?"

"The legality of it is what I'm questioning, and who authorized it. I'm definitely questioning your theory of a rogue underground network that is hidden in the government."

"Well, that remains to be proven. I am with you though; I hope that theory is wrong. I have to retain the concept, however, simply because of the people who are disappearing and dying who shouldn't be. I know about this first hand. I lived to tell about the fertilizer factory, remember? What about Senator Mark Collins? Doesn't that strike you as out of the ordinary? His death shows me that I'm on the right track."

"Well, I see your point, but I still want to reject the whole thing as unreal."

"It is unreal, that is how they are getting away with it. No one would believe it."

"Okay, Zeb, I have to leave now. My plane is waiting. I'll see you in a couple of hours." He hung up and I settled back and waited for his arrival.

A few hours later, he and his wife arrived at the resort. They went to their quarters and spent the rest of the day relaxing. I went for a walk and ended up at the main building. After I had my evening meal, I went back to my cabin and bedded down for the evening. I did not bother the general that evening with my theories or plans. I was concerned that I may sound abnormal to him and his wife if I carried on too strongly about it. They needed their free time together, and I respected that.

In the morning, I did meet up with them in the dining area. I tried to avoid talking about going to Los Alamos, but it needed covered. I slowly introduced the subject into our breakfast conversation.

"So, Mr. Dasher, what are your plans for your future?" The general's wife asked.

"I would like to be able to continue as an investigator."

"Oh, I see. So, what are you going to investigate? From what I understand, that may not be possible."

"That is what is being counted on, but I'm not planning on giving up."

"Don't you think you have investigated enough, and it's time to move on? If what you think and say is true, if you continue, you will surely be killed."

'Well, that is the chance I'm taking. I do it for my country as well as my own personal self-satisfaction. I desire to see this thing through."

"So, what is your next step?" she asked.

"I would like the general, your husband, to arrange for us to go to Los Alamos. We need to be able to look into their files."

"That is probably a tall order. Los Alamos is not open to just anyone. I can get in, but you may be restricted to just a visitor tour. Your ability to investigate would be reduced to slim to none." The general said. "Maybe, I can get some sort of clearance."

"That would be great. This may be about the only way we will be able to see what is happening. So, see what you can do, my friend." I said. We left and went back to our rooms. In a few hours, I got a call from the general.

"Zeb, Coleman here, we're all set. We leave for Arizona tomorrow morning at seven. They will be expecting us. The misses will be staying here until we get back. After that, she and I will be going back to Texas. What you do after that is up to you. I managed to get you a special high clearance ID with your picture on it along with a new name. The ID will be special delivered to me later this evening. I will give it to you in the morning. Your new name is Alex Bacon. Therefore, Alex, get some sleep tonight, and I will be seeing you in the morning. Meet me in the main building's lobby."

"Wow, thank you. I'll be ready to go, so, yes, I'll see you." I hung up the phone and went to bed. I had some difficulty getting to sleep. I was too deep into my thoughts to sleep but after several hours of tossing and turning, I finally fell asleep.

In the morning, after breakfast, we left in a rented car from the resort. Coleman drove us to the nearest airport, which was actually quite a distance. He had a private plane waiting for us at the airport, and we were up and on our way to Arizona in no time. I found that Los Alamos was fairly small, which surprised me. I expected a busy city. This town had its own character that included the housing for former A-bomb scientists, and high fences. When we came up to the gate to the facility, I felt like I was a high school student out on a field trip. The men at the gates checked our credentials and we were escorted in to the welcoming center. We had to wait a while before we were granted further entrance into the facilities. The assistant director of projects was to come out to talk with us and show us various things into which the general had inquired. If all went as planned and the assistant director was open and forthcoming, we would have our answers and be done here.

Shortly, the assistant director showed up, a Dr. Johnathan Goosh. He was accompanied by two armed soldiers, and one MP. After greeting us, he began asking questions about just why we were at Los Alamos. He questioned my credentials, and then, our lack of written authorization from the Defense Department for such a visit. General Cook did have a fax from the Joint Chiefs giving him permission for a visit of inquiry. Dr. Goosh looked at the faxed paper, and apologized for the precautionary delay. He stated that he rarely got any kind of visit from a military general. He claimed that he was just a little curious about the visit.

"We are glad that you have taken the time to come our way, General Cook and you ranking team specialist, Mr. Norman Bacon. Come, Let us get started. I will briefly show you around and then, we will cover any questions that you may have. We would like to extend our hospitality to you both to share dinner here with us later today." Dr. Goosh said, and we followed him out the welcome center's front door to the next building.

27

Success has Its Price

THE GENERAL AND I WALKED into the next building that was a large office building with several desks and rows of filing cabinets in the first room.

Dr. Goosh asked, "Now, gentlemen, how may I help you today?"

"I need your files on a certain project. It is called X Caliber Ten."

"X Caliber Ten?" Dr. Goosh paused, and then said, "I'm afraid that I've never heard of that program, sir. Are you sure that this facility has worked on it?"

"No sir, not really. From what I understand, its point of origin is here, sir. Would it be perhaps by another name?"

"Well, it's possible since I've never heard of what you are asking for."

"Here, let me describe it to you maybe that would help."

"It is worth a try, go ahead."

"This is a nuclear weapon mounted on a super hyper sonic missile that is a nation killer. It throws out multiple warheads that are dirty bombs as it passes over a nation. The warheads are guided and have their own propulsion systems once released. Just one missile could destroy not just a city but also an entire nation. As far as I know, these things are land based, but I am not certain that they didn't find their way into the submarine fleet."

"Dirty bombs? I think we are talking about a weapon system that would be not permitted by our nuclear proliferation treaties."

"Exactly. That is why I am here. Is such a thing being both developed and deployed behind the backs of the American public?"

"That is an interesting question, sir, but one that is probably best answered by the Department of Defense, not me. I know nothing about such a program. Believe me, if such a weapon were being developed here, I would know about it. I am afraid that you have made your trip here for no reason. I'm sorry that I can't help you."

"So, you have no file to show me?"

"No, there is nothing here like what you are describing, and never was."

"Not even under a different code name?"

"Not even under a different code name. Now, if you will excuse me, I must be going about my business. We do develop new systems and test them for reliability here, but no nation killers, sir. Thank you for your attention to that matter. It would be an important thing to investigate if it were true, but there is not any truth in the matter. Good day." Dr. Goosh shook both our hands and showed us the door.

As we walked back to our car, we both noticed a strange looking rocket sitting in a near-by field in the compound. It looked like they were working on mounting some sort of capsule to it.

"I wonder what that is." I asked.

"Whatever it is, it isn't X Caliber Ten, according to Dr. Goosh," Coleman replied.

"Do you have binoculars by some chance?" I asked.

"No, we could probably get a pair in town, why?"

"I would like to take a closer look at what is going on after we leave. Could you drop me off a little ways down the road and then go pick up some binoculars for me? We might learn more on our own than what Dr. Goosh is willing to tell us."

"Okay, I'll drop you off right up here, and I'll be back shortly with your binoculars." Coleman stopped at a parking lot that was near to the Los Alamos lab facility. Apparently, it was not being used any longer being in a state of disrepair.

I got out, "I'm going to walk back to the lab fence. I will keep an eye out for you. Hurry back."

"Okay, I'll get you a good pair of binoculars. Do not get caught. Be back soon."

He left and I walked into a grassy field that approached the fenced in facility. I lay down on my stomach and slowly crawled closer to the fence. I could see several workers doing something to the front of the rocket. I needed binoculars to be able to see what they were clearly doing. Until the general got back with the binoculars, I would have to just do the best I could. It was hot just lying there watching and waiting. A half an hour went by and the general had not returned. Then an hour went by. I was worried that something had happened. I got as close to the fence as I could since I did not have the binoculars yet. I could hear what the workers were saying.

"Make sure that shield is on correctly. We do not want any radiation leak. That stuff is deadly. I do not want to glow at night. The wife wouldn't like it." One of them said.

"Right, this thing is supposed to be the most destructive weapon ever built, and I don't want any of it on me!" Another one replied.

"How many more of these are in the pipe line?

"I'm not sure but I think maybe ten more for now."

"That's a lot of potential exterminations. How many nations are they planning on wiping out?"

"I don't know, as many as they want, I guess."

"I don't understand why they need such a thing as this."

"You haven't heard that the best defense is a good offense?"

"This is more than an offense."

"I don't know. I just do my job. It pays well, that's all that matters."

"You are right. What they do with what we make is their business. Ours is to make what they want and get paid, paid well."

So, who is in charge of this project anyway? I heard that it is the U.N."

"I haven't heard, but that makes sense. If they want world peace, they have to have a peace maker for back-up."

"This one here that we are working on is smaller than some of the others. It must go on a ship of some type."

"That's what I'm thinking."

Therefore, now I was pointed, at last in the right direction. The U.N. was behind the weapon of mass destruction. When fully integrated into a command system, there would be no country that could object to U.N. decisions. So, if this came about, the United States would lose its sovereignty and just be a puppet to the general assembly of the U.N. Even though the weapons were on our soil, we would not have control over them. This would mean U.N. soldiers would be on our soil. I did not like the idea. As far as I was concerned, our mission here was a success, even without obtaining a file.

As I lay there in the dirt, beside the fence, a military vehicle pulled up and stopped in front of me, on my side of the fence. Dr. Goosh got out of the passenger side and walked over to me.

"We have been observing you on our security cameras for quite some time. I am here to tell you some bad news. General Coleman Cook has been killed in an automobile accident just a few minutes ago. He was pronounced dead at the scene."

"General Cook is dead?" I said as I stood up.

"Yes, now if you will get in the vehicle we will take you to our detention center. There are two arresting officers in the vehicle that will cuff you, so if you will kindly just get in, it will all be done peacefully."

"Wait a minute, I'm a private citizen, and the military can't arrest me."

"Sir, you are wanted on espionage charges by the federal government. There are two pending murder charges that you will be facing also."

"Murder charges?"

'"Seems like you are wanted for questioning in the murder of Senator Mark Collins, and for a CIA agent named Rick Hasselbon."

"Mark Collins? Rick is dead?"

"Now, if you will peacefully come with me, we will get on with the inevitable."

"Inevitable?"

28.

Erased and Forgotten

"Guilty on all charges," the judge said and slammed his gavel.

Therefore, that was that. I was found guilty of espionage on multiple counts with their "indisputable proof" that was supplied by the FBI. They said that they had plans to investigate me further into the disappearance of special agent Norman Bacon, and Clyde Ryner! So, they were actually investigating the disappearance of myself. I guess I will be convicted of that too! I was sent to the federal prison in Atwater, California. Ironically, the prison was built on the old Air Force Castle Nuclear Weapons Base.

I am kept in a single maximum-security cell with no visitors, not even attorney visits. I was given a government defense attorney for each case, but he seemed to be more on the government's side than on my side of the arguments. I was not permitted the option of hiring my own attorney. Attorney Jim Thompson, my court appointed attorney, seemed sympathetic to me, but his arguments were weak and ineffective. The public was not invited to the trials. I have no contact with the outside world whatsoever. There were no phone calls were permitted. I am given my food through the slot in the door, and when given a break to go outside, I am cuffed and escorted out to a private section where no one else is permitted. Apparently, I am considered to be one of the most dangerous prisoners in the facility.

My usual guard, an officer Henry Waters, seems to be rather unstable in his treatment of me. One day he is friendly and polite, even verging on nice, but on other days, he is hateful and ridicules me. The hateful days seem to be more regular and common than the good days. The days and nights all blurred together after a while. I didn't any longer know how long I had been in prison, was it months or years? I lost track of time.

"Come on Slim, it's time to go outside for a few minutes. Sunshine you know. Not that you deserve sunshine or anything, but your lord and keeper dictates it. Up and out!" Officer Waters said as he swung open my heavy steel door. As soon as I stepped out of the door the guard put cuffs on my wrists. "If you try any funny stuff you will be cuffed on the ankles also. Don't lose the privileges that you have." He side and gave me a shove toward the door going to the outside.

My exercise area was only an outdoor area twenty feet square with solid walls on all sides that were thirty feet high. I had no hope or thought of trying to escape. For me, hope was gone. I had no idea of what was going on in the outside world. I had no friends left alive that I knew of. I was an only child and my parents were both dead. Therefore, I had no one. I was denied any appeal or possibility of a future parole. All of my plans that I had for my future, my retirement and trips to Europe, all of that was hopelessly gone.

"Okay, buddy, times up. Let's go back in," Officer Waters said and pointed me in the direction of the door. When I got back to the cell, I found my attorney Jim Thompson there waiting for me.

"Okay, you have ten minutes with your attorney," Waters said and slammed the door shut.

Attorney Thompson sat down on the end of the bed, and began, "Good news, I went through the warden and the Federal Board of Corrections, and there's a chance that I can get you out of this prison."

"Out of here and into some other prison? What's the difference?"

"I'm not talking about going to another prison. I'm talking about going to a hospital. The conditions will be much better. You will have interaction with other people, and you can even have visitors.

"Interaction with insane people don't you mean? You are talking about sending me to a mental institution for the rest of my life, aren't you?"

"Well, if you are legally pronounced insane, you will be out of here. Once in a mental hospital, then we can work on the strategy of getting you better. It just may be a way out."

"I don't like it." I said.

"It's all you've got, Zeb. You have no options. There are possible murder accusations of Norman Bacon, and Clyde Ryner. Those may just go away if there are no bodies found. I think they lack evidence for any conviction in either case."

"Don't they just supply the needed evidence?"

'No comment, sir. So, will you give me the go ahead to pursue this course of action?"

"You mean to have me proclaimed insane?"

" Right, you will be examined by the prison psychologist, as well as several federal ones. Just act irrational and stupid and you will be alright."

"I can do that. So, yes, go ahead with your plan. It just may work."

"Right now, you don't even exist any longer, but maybe we can change that."

"What do you mean I don't exist?"

"Your name does not appear on the prison's list of detainees. There's only a number assigned to this cell."

"Interesting."

"I'll get this thing going immediately. You will be visited by several authorities in psychology so you know what to do." Jim Thompson said and left the cell.

Months rolled by and no one came to see me. Then, one day a doctor was admitted to my cell who asked me questions that I thought were strange. I made sure I answered them incorrectly with a blank expression on my face. He left abruptly. I knew then, that my attorney had not let me down. Several months later, two other doctors visited me, one right after the other. I acted dazed and confused. They also left after they questioned me for a few minutes. Some of the questions I left unanswered. I figured that it was important to also act in a stultified manner around the guards. Officer Waters noticed the change in my behavior and seemed to think that I was just losing it.

The best I can tell, it was about three months later that I was stood up in front of a board of men sitting behind a long desk. I was asked about ten questions before they conferred with one another. Then, I heard their verdict:

"Prisoner 134792, by the unanimous decision of this board of inquiry, we do hereby declare you to be totally incompetent in your mental capacities, and are therefore not responsible for your actions. We now will present our recommendations to the governor of this state as well the U.S. Attorney General to have you transferred to a mental institution of their recommendation. You are dismissed. Guards take him away."

Two guards took me back to my cell to wait for my transfer, which occurred a month later. Now, I am in a nameless mental institution, but I hope that will not be forever. Those who run this place seem determined to keep me here. Someday I will get my name back as well as my life. I fear for my country that I will continue to slip away and become some sort of oligarchy. Someday Zeb Dasher the great investigator will have his vengeance when I reveal the truth of what is really going on. It may take time, but time is what God has graciously given us. Yes, I will be free again to fight for the freedoms of my nation that are guaranteed by its Constitution. Until then, I remain erased and forgotten as only 134792.

Don't miss out!

Visit the website below and you can sign up to receive emails whenever Dr. Myron Baughman publishes a new book. There's no charge and no obligation.

https://books2read.com/r/B-A-JHNQB-JDDOD

BOOKS2READ

Connecting independent readers to independent writers.

Did you love *The Strange Case of the Missing Bridge*? Then you should read *Pneumasites*[1] by Myron Baughman!

Ben Benard, after losing his family, is thrown into a strange new world, where he is opposed by interesting but dangerous characters and forces. He finds that his old world has been infected by horrible parasites that threaten the entire population of the earth. In a series of attempts, he struggles against multiple dangerous opponents. By doing so he and his team are flung to the farthest edges of space and time. His quest for answers results in many twists and thought-provoking turns to a surprise ending that will keep you wanting more.

Read more at https://www.sermonaudio.com/source_detail.asp?sourceid=kingjamesseminary.

---

1. https://books2read.com/u/mV27GP

2. https://books2read.com/u/mV27GP

Also by Dr. Myron Baughman

The Strange Case of the Missing Bridge

Watch for more at https://www.sermonaudio.com/
source_detail.asp?sourceid=kingjamesseminary.

About the Author

Dr. Myron Baughman is a popular author and speaker with several books on the active market: Pneumasites 1 & 2, both science fiction novels, and children's books: My Puppy Theo, and Trixie the Pixie Angel. being the most recent. Dr. Baughman is married with four children and lives in Georgia, U.S.A.

Read more at https://www.sermonaudio.com/source_detail.asp?sourceid=kingjamesseminary.